SHEILA CHILSON

ISBN
978-1-956161-41-0 (Hardcover)
978-1-956161-40-3 (Paperback)
978-1-956161-39-7 (eBook)

Prologue

The strong winds of a nor'easter came blowing across Lake Ontario and entered Central New York with snow and hail covering everything in its path. The high wind sounded like a freight train as it advanced around and over the three silos. The stone structures stood like soldiers guarding the hilltop from the advancing menace. The lonely howling of the wind filled Jack with the "what ifs" of this past year. His divorce was one. He missed Tess and his great kids. He also felt deep sadness at the murders of the best in-laws anyone could ever have.

He never would have agreed to being the head of the Homeland Committee Seven if he had realized the danger that would destroy his marriage and put them all at risk, much less involve his father-in-law. The plan to find ways to help rural America to defend itself against terrorism had started out as an investigative committee, not a doing committee.

Operation Silo had developed out of Jack's obsession to repair the three historical silos built on Tess's family farm. In the early 1850s, Italian stonemasons were brought to New York State to build the Erie Canal. Many amazing limestone homes and business and farm buildings were built by these wonderful masons of the past. The unique structures have stood the test of time and can be seen all over the northern United States.

As Jack traveled to committee meetings by car or plane, he noticed the many silos and grain storage bins all over America.

They were everywhere, some in use and some obviously neglected. One day his curiosity started developing into an idea that turned into a plan. He called his research assistant to glean information on farm families and their connection to the military. Jack's idea was a winner. The research showed that 87 percent of farm families had one or more members in active or part-time service in one of the branches of the of the United States military. They were by and large land-loving patriots. Doing that research accomplished step one. Step two was to divide the country into designated areas that could be used as distribution points for groups of people. Step three was locating the right citizens in these areas to hide and protect the secret stash of weapons. Step four was the repair and remodeling of silos to turn them into miniature armories. They would be scattered throughout the sparsely populated countryside of America. Delivery of weapons would be easy to disguise by using large cattle or horse trailers. These haulers were always in and about the small towns of rural America. No one would ever question deliveries made to farms by an animal hauler.

The committee immediately agreed that this was a workable project. Notifications would be sent to the farms that had met the specific qualifications. Then the silos could be overhauled inside and out. New electric wiring, temperature control, computer equipment, and sophisticated security measures would be put in place. Some of the silos had offices and living quarters installed in the upper portions of the huge structures. It made life easier for the people responsible for the weapons.

Jack had been put on alert about Internet chatter coming from the Middle East. They were searching for information about guns and ammunition being shipped out of military facilities with no traceable trail. The Committee Seven members were all tight-lipped, security-conscious military types. But somehow the assassins had learned of Frank's involvement in the secret Committee Seven. These foreign thugs had broken into Frank and Mary's home in Florida and murdered the seventy-five-year-old patriots. The couple had not gone quietly. There was blood at the scene that was not Frank's or Mary's.

Jack would forever miss these two beloved people.

1

Tess felt chilled in mind and body. It wasn't the crisp autumn air on this October morning that made her shiver. Quick-change weather was one of many things Central New Yorkers loved about their state. The soft, hazy sun could be warming Tess as she started the morning barn chores and would peel off her work jacket. Then fast-traveling clouds would roll across Lake Ontario from Canada, picking up tons of condensed water droplets. Twirling windstorms on this huge freshwater lake would push and shove the heavy, low-moving clouds across its surface in a battle of nature's weather patterns. The snow-filled clouds would travel for hundreds of miles before wind, weight, and time made them drop their heavy load of glistening white stuff. The icy winds traveling in front of the snow would push the warm air to a distant place. Tess could stand at the thermometer and watch the temperature drop by twenty degrees. She would be pulling on the discarded jacket and wrapping her scarf a little snugger around her neck from the chilly change. She loved to look at the feathery ice designs, some flakes as large as a dime, as they floated past her nose. Driving a car down the back roads to her farm was another matter during one of these winter snow blasts. The county snowplow trucks always worked the main roads first then plowed and salted the secondary roads as the storms slowed in intensity. Lots of times, it was hard for Tess to tell the difference between her driveway and the harvested cornfield road that ran beside it.

Not much snow had fallen this morning. Today it was tears caused by her broken heart that obscured her path to home. Tess and Jack had signed on the dotted line. The divorce of their twenty-one-year marriage was official. Their nineteen-year-old twin sons, Tom and Jamie, were away at college. Their sixteen-year-old daughter, Sara, would be home shortly on the school bus.

The coming of cold weather and the shorter days of the season always marked the beginning of a reduction in outside time. There would not be lawn or pasture to mow or flowers and garden to enjoy. The soft, silent snow chased people and animals inside for shelter from the harsh, howling wind and freezing temperatures. You read the books that working in the garden had kept you from. There was old movie night for family and friends. Cooking became entertainment for the whole clan to help with in the preparation of a snack or feast. The hostile environment outside was an unwelcome world to the ill-prepared. Everyone in the path of the lake-effect weather pattern of New York State had no choice but to go for the warm and cozy of inside time.

Today, Tess didn't go into the house for another cry but instead walked to the large dog kennel by the side of the barn. She opened the gate and let Barley and Sam out for a run. Tess hadn't realized how large Bernese mountain dogs could grow.

She had seen her girls for the first time at her favorite pet shop in town. She had gone into the store to buy the family canary, Tweety, his favorite birdseed. These little yellow birds had been singing in the kitchen of her family's farmhouse for over a hundred years. This tiny fellow was Tweety number seventeen. Tess's mother and grandmother had always loved the sweet songs these little singers sang. Tess was carrying on the canary tradition.

As Tess walked into the small pet shop, she spotted two pups in a large pen in the center of the store. There was a handwritten paper sign on the side of the pen that said: Bernese Mountain Pups Special. She had to stop and give the two babies a rub. Their baby skin and hair was silky soft. Their color markings were the usual shiny black, reddish-brown, and crisp white of their breed. At ten weeks of age, their weight was already over twenty pounds. Tess walked away from the cute pups and went to the back of the store in the hunt for Tweet's favorite seed and treats.

The puppies started desperately calling with sharp little yaps for Tess to come back while jumping up and down on the side of their pen. Tess gathered the seed bags and walked up a side aisle to keep from looking at the puppies' desperate faces. As she paid for her purchases, Tess asked a few questions about the pups. The young checkout girl told her: "They are sisters and are ten weeks old. They are vet-checked and up to date on vaccinations."

Tess said, "Just add them to my card."

Out came Tess carrying the twenty-pound girls, one under each arm, along with the bag of Tweety's seed and treats.

They were now four years old, and her gentle giants were in the 175-pound range each. They were Tess's shadow when she was home, and it was common to see two big, shaggy heads hanging out either side of the backseat windows of Tess's farm truck.

Tess opened the gate to the pasture, and the happy girls ran down the hill for a quick release of their unlimited energy. She stood for a moment to watch their wild rush to the woods in an excited chase of a bouncing squirrel. It made her think how scary it would feel to be chased by animals as large as her guardians. The squirrel made it to a limb at the top of a tall oak tree. It started the squirrel cursing and chattering from its high, safe position as the two dogs threw themselves into a frenzy of jumping up and down at the base of the tree with shrieks of murderous baying. The squirrel danced back and forth with its threats of what he would do to the girls if they made it up to his safe haven.

With a welcome laugh at the animal antics, Tess turned to start her afternoon chores.

The large two-story barn her grandfather and dad had built many years ago with the help of Amish carpenters was Tess's favorite place in the world. Her dad was just a young teenager when a winter storm took the original 1840s barn structure down. So the men built this huge new barn to be a shelter from the storms of the seasons and a fine seat in the shade.

The big dogs had finished their run and come back to be close to Tess. They sensed her sadness and gently rubbed against her in catlike fashion as she moved around the barn. Tess put a scoop of cracked corn and pellet feed with vitamins in the chicken feed pans and changed the drinking water. She counted the number of hens and collected the eggs in the same basket her mother and grandmother had used before turning the job over to Tess. She made sure everyone was accounted for and then closed the gate for the day.

Tess fed all of her animals twice a day and did a nighttime check before bed. She looked them over with her time-trained eye for anything that might become a problem. Her grandfather and father were both doctors of veterinarian medicine. They had also served their country as food inspectors and cared for military service dogs. The father-and-son team had worked with Doctors Without Borders to help educate poverty-stricken areas of the world on the raising and caring of farm animals. Tess had been expected to follow in their footsteps. But Tess's heart had always been in teaching—and, more importantly, in teaching what made Americans and the United States great.

The horses were down in the pasture but heard the familiar sound of Tess's car. They came at a fast trot up the hill and saw her walking toward the barn. The horses entered the open back door of their individual barn stalls and started calling Tess with soft neighs and occasional stomps of a foot. They were eagerly awaiting a slice of apple or a horse cookie from their favorite person. Tess didn't shut them in their stalls this early in the season. They came into the barn or went out to the pasture as they pleased until the weather worsened. The four red roan quarter horse mares were Tess's treasurers. They won many trophies at the state and national horse shows for their wonderful conformation. They also had amazing dispositions – not a troublemaker was in the group.

Then there was Zane, the stallion. He was the most beautiful animal Tess ever had the honor to own. He was as black as the darkest night. His regal stance and great temperament made him a true prize. Tess looked them over as she cooed softly to each one, telling them how beautiful and special they each were. There was nothing to compare to a warm nuzzle from the soft nose of a horse friend.

Tess was feeling better already. The not knowing was much worse than the finality of signing the divorce papers. Declaring herself in charge of her own life and not responsible for Jack's happiness was a relief. For the moment, the tightness was gone from her body. She was satisfied with the fact that she had worked hard to save her marriage. You can't have an answer for a problem you don't understand. Tess declared this day, October 27, to be Freedom Day.

As Tess stood at the back door of the barn and looked out across the rolling pastures and woods beyond, she could see the tops of the three silos standing tall and stately. The tall cylinder structures stood like sentinels with their beautiful slate roofs shining in the afternoon sun. Jack had insisted on having them repaired seven years ago. He and Tess had quit the argument about the wisdom of spending money on farm buildings that weren't being used anymore. Jack's stand was that the silos were historical structures. They had been built by Italian stonemasons who had come to America to build the Erie Canal back in the early 1800s. Jack wanted them repaired to their original specifications. All Tess could think about was that college expenses were coming soon for the boys. But Jack never ran out of words and Tess couldn't find enough of them to explain her thoughts. So she settled for peace and quiet in her barn. The three silos would stand tall and proud for another 180 years, marking the hilltop corner of her farm.

Tess had not gone to look at the repairs done to the silos. The structures weren't easy to get to from the house. They had been built on a tall, flat hill on the farthest southwestern corner of her farm. Getting to the silos with huge farm tractors and loaded grain wagons was made easier by using a paved county-maintained road that ran parallel to the back line of her farm. The trucks and tractors would turn off the county road and onto a narrow half-mile dirt road that Jack had always kept graded and hole free for the big equipment. The farm road led thru shady woods and curved to the left at the hundred- acre field. Then you traveled another mile and a half to the loading chutes of the enormous silos. The wagons of fresh picked corn and other grains would be hydraulically sucked into the silos. Inside the silos, huge fans and heaters would blow and dry the grain for the coming winter. The big fans and heaters ran day and night in grain bins all over America this time of year.

The rumbling trucks would come down the same road to reload the dried grain to deliver it to companies who turned it into food for animals and people. Tess enjoyed hearing the low purr of the fans and motors from this distance. Up close to the silos, the sound became more of a roar.

If you wanted to go to the silos by horse or four-wheelers, you had to travel over a mile through the horse and cattle pastures, stopping to open several heavy gates that separated the fields. From this point you entered forty acres of woods that sloped down sharply. Jack and the boys kept the trails mowed for wonderful fun times of lazy afternoon rides by horse or for the wild fast rides on the noisy quads.

The winding forest trail ended at a deep, fast-moving creek that divided the farm in half. The crossing was always questionable, depending on rain or snow melt. In the winter, the stream was a sheet of ice. It was impossible to cross it safely. You could never guess where to step or guide a horse or quad, because the moving water kept the icy surface unstable. When you made it over the stream, there was a tough climb up a rocky, steep hill. At the top of the hill, you came to a hundred acres of corn, or whatever the farmer Tess rented the land to was growing. The silos were on the far side of this field. Jack had built a ten-foot fence with locked gates around the silos, and Tess didn't even have a key.

Jack had asked in the divorce agreement to use one of the silos for storage of his personal things. Tess didn't mind. She had no use for the silos.

She stepped out of her barn with the thought of a strong cup of hot tea and maybe a bowl of that soup she had made yesterday. The flavor of homemade soup made from the fresh herbs Tess picked from her garden by the kitchen door was always tastier the following day. It was less than an hour before she would leave to teach her afternoon and evening classes at the community college.

The snowfall had stopped, leaving just a white dusting on the ground and treetops. The sun's last warm glow kissed Tess's upturned face. Everything around her—the house and fifteen hundred acres of fields and forest—was hers by inheritance. Tess had her master's degree in pre-law and her doctorate in political science. She had been teaching political science at Cayuga County College for thirteen years. It started as a part-time teaching spot when Sara entered first grade. With all three children in school, Tess finally had time to fulfill her first love, teaching.

Tess had the respect of her students, who enjoyed her classes. There was always a waiting list of students eager to learn from her. She shared world information and ideas of democracy with young minds. These young people would go out into the world with an understanding of the importance of freedom and keeping America safe.

Her parents wanted the farm to stay in the family. Being an only child brought a certain pressure to produce heirs, and Tess had accomplished this beautifully. Her mom and dad had loved Jack and enjoyed their three beautiful grandchildren. It was the biggest blow in Tess's life when ten months ago her parents had been murdered by robbers in their Florida home.

Tess's mom and dad had come to New York for their yearly month-long visit with Tess and her family. They were deeply upset by the surprise of Tess and Jack being separated. Her father had spent a lot of time alone with Jack, talking privately about the situation. Tess was starting to feel that her Dad was being disloyal to her. Following each of her father's visits with Jack, Tess's dad would come back home, not angry, but seeming more resolved that divorce was the best answer for all of their problems. After one such visit with Jack, her father hugged Tess tightly, and mumbled over her shoulder, that he just wanted Tess and his grandchildren to be safe. Tess had not understood, but her Dad would not talk about it.

Tess did not have to depend on Jack for money or her life decisions. His inability to share his thoughts or activities started about four years ago when Jack walked up to her in the barn and out of nowhere said: "I need to be gone for a few weeks. Don't ask me any questions. You can handle everything here." She had been stunned. It was the first in a series of "I'm not going to talk about it because I'm too busy" no-detail conversations that stopped their marriage and started their divorce.

Jack missed his home, his wife, and his family. Besides being brilliant, beautiful, and an amazing woman, Tess was a great cook. He always loved walking into the house to the smell of her apple cobbler baking. The delicious cinnamon scent wafting from the kitchen to all parts of the house was almost as good as her kiss hello. *Almost.*

He had stayed with his family too long. Their safety was the most important thing to him. He could mend fences with them later. The silos were now his only connection to the farm. At least he was still standing on the same hallowed ground Tess loved so much: America – her home, her country.

Jack, like Tess, was an only child born to older parents that had given up the thought of being blessed with a child. Jack and his parents had lived all over the world. His father served as ambassador to India, Pakistan, and finally Africa. His mother was a well-respected eye surgeon who donated her time and energy helping people of whatever country her husband was serving.

They had no time to bake Jack an apple pie. He attended private boarding school with a wide variety of boys from prominent and usually wealthy families. It was a diverse ethnic group. Jack learned much about respecting other people's beliefs, but more importantly about standing up for his own country and Christian beliefs.

When Jack graduated from prep school at seventeen, his dad told him, "Son, it is time for you to learn why America is the greatest country in the world. It's time for us to go home." After twenty-seven years of his parents' service and seventeen years of Jack's life, they were ready to kiss the American soil when they arrived at the family home. Jack loved the rolling hills and valleys with the beautiful clear lakes in tree-lined valleys that went on for miles all over Central New York. You were never bored on a road trip with the amazing scenery. He and his parents were happy and relaxed in their home in Syracuse.

When fall came, Jack began college at his parents' alma mater, Syracuse University. Then he met Tess, and the rest (he thought) would be history. It would have been, if dangerous hot spots of terrorist cells had not started cropping up in unexpected places in the world. They all seemed to have the destruction of America as their first priority. Jack had to help protect America, to keep his family safe.

So on this night, Jack became a lonely sentinel on the hill, scanning Tess's house and grounds with his night vision binoculars. The deep amber glow of the harvest moon lit up the scene below. The trees and long distances between Jack and his family prevented him from feeling like much of a protector for Tess and Sara. The old farm's layout looked like a miniature dollhouse. A soft glow began in the house as lights were turned on in the kitchen and den. Tess and Sara would prepare the meal together. The evening dinner was always a close family time to share the good and the bad of the day. Sara's homework would be discussed, and if she needed help, Tess would sit down with Sara and they would get the job completed.

The lights went on and off with Tess and Sara's movements throughout the house. The girls moved to their bedrooms on the second floor. They took their baths and climbed into their beds for a few phone calls and maybe a chapter or two of a good book to relax before sleep. Jack scanned what he could from such a great distance of the back boundaries of the house and surrounding yard and barn areas. He had been informed by the FBI that Internet terrorist chatter had increased. The army was concerned that those terrorists were trying to glean information about the weapons projects. It seems that Jack's name came up in some of the chatter. This was the fear Jack had for his family. He had to settle for what comfort he could get from the knowledge that Tess had a handgun in her nightstand and that Barley and Sam stayed in the house at night. The big dogs would kill for Tess and Sara.

Good people don't expect or understand evil. They don't start with a level playing field. Tess's parents had not been fast enough to survive their attackers. There was plenty of evidence that they had put up quite a fight. The seventy-five-year-old beloved grandparents had time to use a handgun against the thugs and call 911 before the monsters murdered them. Jack would never stop missing his wonderful in-laws.

The muffled beeping of Jack's cell phone interrupted his thoughts and his watch of home. He got the okay to proceed with his delivery.

Jack had done more than just repair the silos. The three had identical repairs done to the slate roofs and tile siding. They were already equipped with water, gas, and electricity for the drying and storing of grain. He just expanded the wiring to power the emergency generators and satellite connections for communication with the army division he was working with. The silo in the back of the row, farthest from the road, was equipped with many more specialties on the inside. Jack had an office and a two-story living area with all the comforts of a home away from home. His silo had a small attached barn that concealed his truck, car, and trailers. It was quite unsuspicious-looking to the outside world. Jack had also insisted on the ten-foot security fence for the protection of the historical structures, and no one questioned him. He and the semiretired army sergeant farmer that rented the fields from Tess had the keys. He also worked under Jack to distribute weapons to the Midwest.

Jack was delivering this load of weapons to a prepared farm in Pennsylvania. The orange glow from the moon cast an eerie pallor on the frosty, silver ribbon of endless road in front of him. He drove four hours on highway 81 and then exited at the town of Skull Kill, Pennsylvania. The long, heavy-duty horse trailer that his 350 Ford Dully truck was pulling through the mountains was loaded with automatic rifles, handguns, and enough ammo to start a war or end one. The United States Army assigned Jack the secret mission of establishing the logistics and delivery of weapons to central locations in each state. They would all be hidden on private land, so they could be placed in the hands of Middle Americans if war happened. Jack was in charge of directing the mission all over the United States, and he was also delivering weapons to areas from the top of Maine and down the western side of New York State.

Who better to trust with the safekeeping of America than hard-working, land-loving farmers? Silos are a constant on any farm, large or small, for grain storage. North, south, east, and west, the sight of silos represents the preparation and readiness for winter. It shows the mindset of farmers all over America. They are thinkers about the future. Another year of feed for the farm animals means another year of food for America's people. The farmers of this land will stand and fight for their neighbors and their country's freedoms. The United States Army is the original minutemen of America.

That's why Jack knew it would work. He would accomplish this job of honor. He would be arming groups of militia with military supplies for a battle that they all hoped would never happen.

Through the grays and blacks of a shadow world cast from a cloudless moon, Jack saw the tall Pennsylvania silos as he rounded a curve in the narrow mountain road. He spotted at least five ghostly figures standing by the reddish glow of a large campfire. They could easily be figures from the past, such as George Washington and his brave band of men. These men were of the same mindset as past heroes who fought for America's freedom. The time had come to stand up for our homeland.

Jack approached the scene with caution. The group of five stepped forward on this frosty evening to make their way into history, maybe not by name, but by the commitment to do the right thing to protect their family and country.

The coffee was hot and strong. The men gathered around the fire and talked in warrior voices. Then they got to work unloading the weapons. It was a holy moment of commitment as they carried the heavy crates of weapons from Jack's trailer to the prepared hiding place in the silos.

Tess got up with the sunrise. Early morning was her favorite alone time – just a warm mug of good coffee and her thoughts. She would think and solve problems in her mind before the day got under way. But there was one problem she would never get over or understand: Jack.

She missed her best friend. It was like an all-over body ache that aspirin can't make better. She thought back to the first time she talked with Jack. She was seventeen and content with her passion of loving her family and her horses. Jack had phoned to speak to her dad about stabling his just-purchased blue roam mare. Tess answered the telephone, and the sound of his voice went from her ear to her heart. It was the same for Jack. He called and called, and they talked and talked.

Tess had a new passion—a handsome law student. Jack was four years older and had almost completed his law degree. Tess's parents wanted her to complete two years of college before they married, so they waited. It had been a good life of commitment, children, and self-growth. But Jack's unexplained change of character sent their marriage on the short, difficult path to a divorce attorney.

Tess heard her daughter, Sara, rumbling around upstairs, getting ready for school. The bus would be coming shortly, and there was always a morning rush for a misplaced book or shoes.

Sara was going to be a good driver. She just needed more snow driving experience. Riding the bus was the safe way to finish one more school year. New York State weather would provide that driving in the snow lesson any time now. Tess wanted to be with Sara to share all her safety tips. The promise of a spring shopping trip to local car dealerships was keeping the dream in reasonable reach for Sara.

Tess had one class on Western world politics to teach at two in the afternoon, and a night class, which started at six thirty. The evening class on Eastern world politics and culture was always exhilarating and usually lasted until nine, so Tess was always home around nine thirty or at the latest ten o'clock.

Tess left dinner on the stove for Sara, who was to phone her as soon as she got home from school. Tonight would be different for both of them.

Tess's afternoon class was exhilarating, with good participation from the students. She was looking forward to the evening class, which was always attended by a few of the local townsfolk and retired military who came for the discussions and to share their knowledge from serving or observing the troubled Islamic hot spots in areas all over the world.

Tess was about twenty minutes into the first portion of the evening class when in walked a lone man in a dark coat and hat. The auditorium style lecture hall's bright lights shone on the podium and Tess. The students were in the lighting that gets dimmer as your line of vision moves to the back of the room. Tess couldn't tell who the latecomer might be.

The lecture got lively with discussions as they advanced into the second portion of the two-hour class. Tess forgot about the stranger long before the class ended. Her thoughts turned to getting home and seeing Sara. She packed her book bag and gathered her purse as different students walked to comment on the night's lecture and say goodnight. Everyone left the classroom quickly.

The outside temperature had been dropping all day. You could feel the frostiness of snow in the air. Tess was just a few minutes behind her students, but the hallway was already empty as she locked her classroom door and headed toward the exit doors to the parking lot. No one was standing around with the usual good-bye chatter. They were ready for the warmth of home, and so was Tess.

Nick, one of the college security guards, always timed his building checks to walk Tess to her car, rain, snow, or shine. As Tess stepped out into the cold night air, there was no Nick. The heavy metal door to the hallway closed behind her with a loud thud. At this time of night, it locked automatically. Snow floated down in a thick, twirling fashion. The sharp, icy wind sucked all the warmth from her body. Tess had never felt afraid before when leaving her class at night, but something was wrong. Suddenly, she snapped into alert mode. The parking lot was empty except for her car. The Mountaineer was about five rows out from the sidewalk and about seven parking spaces over toward the right. The parking lot had been full of cars and people when she parked earlier. She would have to park closer with winter here and no Nick.

Tess headed for her car, leaning into the cold wind and icy snow. She didn't notice the dark van over at the back end of the parking lot. Between her car and the school, she realized that her car keys were somewhere in her bottomless purse. Tess had not put on her gloves, and her half-frozen fingers became clumsy and numb from the icy wind, making it hard for her to tell the car keys from all the other objects that end up in the bottom of a woman's purse.

The dark van came to life and seemed to be floating through the now heavy snowfall. Tess felt a momentary sense of relief when the van drove toward her. It had to be Nick. When she got to her locked car and put her briefcase on the ground, she started searching again through her bag for the elusive keys. But the van pulled up to her— too close, almost pining her against her car. As she turned with a smile for Nick, she found herself looking into the barrel of a gun.

One look at Jack's woman had given Al-K his first-ever feeling of remorse. He had slid the van door open, and the soft interior light shone on her sweet, smiling face. It was easy to see that she had been expecting a friend, not a gun to her face. Al-K had automatically pushed the gun to the spot between her eyes and found himself looking into the most beautiful blue eyes he had ever seen.

Al-K had kidnapped and murdered so many people he had lost count. This was the first time someone's fear had given him physical pain. It was like a knife cutting a hole in his soul. He had never even thought about having a soul till the moment he looked into those eyes. She had seen straight thru him. Her fear was now his fear.

He helped her into the back seat of the van and, in his broken English, told her to buckle her seat belt. Why did he feel the need to say anything to his prisoner? He suddenly felt shaky and started to sweat heavily. He had seen those blue eyes before. But where? Suddenly he remembered. They were the same eyes of the old woman that had shot him in Florida. He and his men had thought they would just break into the old couple's home and beat the information they wanted out of them. But they must have heard them coming. Al-K had to shoot the old man before the old man shot him. Then the woman came out shooting. She shot Al-K twice. One bullet cut a bloody path across his cheek, thru his ear, and then burned its way just under the skin of his neck, leaving a deep, bloody gash that sprayed his blood all over the room. As the bullet left his body, it was still going strong. It entered the hand of one of his men, breaking several bones in his wrist. The other bullet that the grandmother shot at Al-K blew its way deep into his shoulder. He had seen death coming to him from the stare of those intense, deep blue eyes.

One of his men shot her through the heart, or she would have killed Al-K and maybe all of the other men as well. The bullet was still embedded deep in his shoulder. The pain was worst at night. And tonight he realized that old, blue-eyed warrior had been this younger woman's mother.

It was strange for his mind to be affected this way. Al-K hoped he could shake this feeling that made the hair on his arms and neck stand up. He had been raised to believe in superstitious implications of events. He wished he could talk to the old, wise women of his village to get the meaning of his fear of those blue eyes. He had been away from his village too long. It had been almost two years since he had seen his three wives and seven children. The seer of the village might be dead by now. She was over a hundred years old when he last needed her help. Al-K had his first ever twinge of homesickness.

That was what he had seen in both pairs of eyes. It was the look of a fearless warrior protecting her love of home and family.

By eleven thirty, Sara was panicked. Her mom had called as she was leaving her classroom at nine thirty. Tess had told Sara she was stopping on her way home for milk and wanted to know if Sara needed anything for school tomorrow. They had talked for a moment and ended their quick chat with Tess and Sara exchanging "I love you."

Even sitting in the house by herself, Sara felt loved and protected just from hearing those words. She got up and made herself a cup of hot coco. She then covered up on the sofa in front of the television in the den to wait for her Mom. Sara dozed off watching reruns. She suddenly jerked awake with terrible fear, like a punch to her stomach. It was after eleven o'clock, and no Mom. Sara called Tess's cell phone several times, but there was no answer, only empty rings. Sara's tears started. She was still very angry with her dad for leaving their family, but her fears for her mom brought her to her senses.

Jack saw Sara's name on his phone and answered it on the second ring. He gave his usual: "Hi, baby, what's up?" Sara could hardly speak through her tears. Her overwhelming fear was like a heavy pair of hands tightly gripping her throat in a choke hold. Sara struggled to get her words out. She finally blurted out: "Mom hasn't come home from her class—if you even care."

Jack was stunned that Sara thought he didn't care. To hear Tess was two hours late cut him to the core of his soul. He had just pulled up to the silos from another delivery of weapons to Maine. He got out of his truck and climbed into his Jeep. The snow had been coming down hard. He would have to plow snow from the driveways in the morning.

Jack tried to smooth over Sara's fears with small talk while his own fears grew. He told her to stay put in case Tess called or came home and headed out on the route Tess always took to work. He looked at both sides of the road for signs of Tess's car. The roadways were a slippery mess from the heavy, wet snow.

He kept Sara talking and drove as fast as he dared. Jack arrived at the college parking lot where Tess parked for her class. There were flashing lights coming from several local police cars and two New York State trooper units. An ambulance was loading up a heavily blanketed victim.

Jack hung up on Sara as his car slid to a stop in the snow. He jumped out and ran to the ambulance. Nick, the security guard, was having hard chills from hypothermia. He has taken some nasty blows to his face. Jack scanned the group for Tess with no luck. Then he noticed the New York State troopers at a car that looked like Tess's Mountaineer. They were just picking up a briefcase and purse off the snow-covered pavement in front of the driver's door. Jack almost dropped to his knees with fear. His phone started ringing, and Jack was expecting Sara's voice, but instead the voice in his ear was from his past, and it said: "My friend, we have your wife."

Tess was scared. The gun in her face put her into survival mode. The large, burly man holding the gun stepped halfway out of the van and extended his other hand to help Tess into the open sliding door on the passenger side. She had no choice but to cooperate. He told her in broken English to get into the back seat and buckle up, so Tess did.

Two other men were in the van: one the driver, the other sitting in the front passenger seat. Neither looked back at Tess or said a word. The interior light of the van was too dim to see their faces. Tess could tell by the accent of the thug holding the gun that he was Middle Eastern. The others she couldn't guess. Her thoughts got away from her for a moment, and she worried for Jack and Sara's safety. The man who had held the gun to her face called Jack on his cell phone and put it on speakerphone. At first Tess heard the fear in Jack's voice, then a voice she'd never heard from him—red hot with dangerous, aggressive anger. It's a "just let me get my hands on you" sound.

Tess saw a slight tremor start on the hand of the man holding the phone. Jack's words put fear into her kidnapper. Their fear filled Tess with anger and strength.

These men who had taken her at gunpoint and were now threatening Jack appeared to be foreigners. Tess discerned that she was the button they were using to push Jack to do something very wrong, something she had no knowledge of.

Ad ham Al-Awkary knew he had a tiger by a very short tail to be challenging Jack over his wife or country. Al-Awkary had known Jack from the age of ten. They had gone to the same boarding school, a top-notch military school that teaches young men to follow in the footsteps of their parents, mostly politicians or military leaders. The young men were from all over the Eastern part of the world, and most were from elite, wealthy backgrounds. They had been born into the responsibilities of becoming leaders for their home and countries.

Jack did a mind search on the voice he just heard. His brain was on overload as he scanned his memory for a face to match the voice. It took him back to a quiet boy at boarding school in Saudi Arabia. The skinny kid had joined the class two months late. Everyone had already paired off in the small class of fifty with seven ten-year-olds. The skinny kid's name soon got shortened to Al-K. One of Jack's instructors at the school asked Jack to take Al-K under his wing so he could adjust to school life. Jack was always willing to help. He took the quiet boy under his wing and tried to include him in all the school fun times and also help him with studies. Jack had not thought about Al-K since their last handshake at graduation.

Al-Awkary's life had started out differently from the rest of the wealthy, titled young men. He was saved from the streets of Cairo by the wife of a wealthy Arab Prince after his parents were killed by a roadside bomb. Al-K escaped death because, like any child, he had run ahead to get a better look at a herd of goats and sheep crossing the road. He looked back just as his mother stepped on the land mine. There was nothing left of his parents. The goat herders took him into Cairo and left him at the market to beg or die. They had too many children of their own to feed. They could not take on another.

La Maya had passed by the tiny boy seating in the hot sun, drooping against the wall at the entrance to the market. She wasn't sure he was still alive. She did her shopping with her bodyguard-driver and his wife, who followed her down the long isle of stalls loaded with different merchandize. The big man followed the two women closely, holding a large black umbrella over La Maya's head. She had finished shopping much sooner than usual. The nagging worry about the sight of such a small child in terrible distress had distracted her from the enjoyment she always felt from seeing all the amazing fabrics, clothing, and fresh foods at this huge market. Her driver was surprised when she told him she was finished.

As they returned to the car, these three parents of young children had to pass by the silent, tiny figure. La Maya told her driver to go and see if the child was alive. When he went to check, he found him to be breathing, so he asked the front vendors if they knew anything about the boy, but no one did. The market vendors had concluded that the child was an orphan that would not live much longer on the streets of Cairo.

La Maya waited in the car as long as she could control herself. She kept glancing out the window every minute to see if the child was still breathing. She had recently lost a baby who died shortly after being born. She could feel the street orphan's desperate sadness as his short life was coming to an end. Her driver and friend came back to the car and explained to this kind lady what he had learned. La Maya told him to get a blanket from the trunk of the car. When he returned to the child, he wrapped the tiny shivering figure up in the soft cashmere blanket and placed him in the passenger seat in the front of the car. The boy was filthy and covered with lice.

The driver and his wife agreed to take care of the little boy and try to bring him back from near death. La Maya told them to take him to the hospital. She would be responsible for the charges. The boy soon recovered with the excellent care he received at the hospital once the staff learned that La Maya was his benefactor. Physically, he grew rapidly, but he didn't show affection to the people around him. He wasn't mean, did anything he was asked, and even looked for ways to be helpful. But he acted like the joy of life had left him and his spirit was empty.

La Maya, her kind husband, and everyone in the household tried to give him affection. Al-Awkary was not able or maybe did not want to become attached to anyone. This adopted family wanted the best for him. La Maya's husband decided to send him to the boarding school that he had attended as a young man. And that is how Al-K came to know Jack.

Al-Awkary never thought in a million years he would be challenging this tough American. All the students in school had admired Jack, who had a way about him that made you feel protected as long as you were doing the right thing. You knew if you went the wrong way in the treatment of other students or cocked an attitude, you would lose the friendship and kindness this young American seemed to radiate. Everyone wanted to be Jack's friend. They knew he was capable of great leadership. It is always wise to be in alliance with a shining star. Al-Awkary quaked in his boots.

Tess sat in the back of the van, trying to see out the side windows. The night was a dark whirl of heavy snow, and she couldn't get her sense of direction. If there was a moon or stars that night, they couldn't shine through the winter blast. The trio had not spoken to her, so Tess was left to her own thoughts. They had not tied her up or even threatened her since she was helped into the back of the van.

Tess pulled her coat closer to fight the chill and fear. She felt a slight, hard bulge in her coat pocket—her cell phone. She had put it in her pocket after talking to Sara and felt it come to life against her hip. Luckily, she had put it on vibrate while she was teaching.

The van traveled about forty-five minutes west on the thruway toward Rochester. They exited, glided through the EZ-Pass lane, and turned north. Twenty-five minutes later, they turned right onto a lit entrance with large, black metal gates and a guard. The van traveled about two hundred feet down a curving driveway lined with brightly glowing lampposts and came to a stop in front of a very large house. A veiled woman opened the front door of the house, and the two men in the front of the van got out and went inside. The man seated in front of Tess slowly turned around and gave her a silent stare.

Tess never moved or returned his look. Al-Awkary is the one who felt the chill run down his spine. He opened the van door and told her to get out. He took her arm as if to the help her out of the van, but took a stiffer hold as she stepped out into the heavy blowing snowstorm. He later told the others that Tess's eyes glowed bright red as she looked at him through the snowy darkness.

Tess felt a slight tremor from Al-K's hand on her arm as she met his look again. No words passed between them as he guided her up the icy steps and into the brightly lit entrance of a beautiful turn-of-the-century mansion. The floors were polished gray and white marble. Huge oriental rugs in deep reds and indigo blue made a path to closed double doors leading to the back of the home.

Al-K led Tess to the amazing mahogany staircase, which curved elegantly up to the third floor. A huge chandelier glowed softly high up on the top floor ceiling. A strong, icy gust of loud, wailing wind from the storm entered with Tess and Al-K. It whirled all around them, feeling like ghostly fingers pulling and playing with their clothing and hair. It traveled up the staircase to the top of the vaulted ceiling and created a sharp, twinkling tune on the crystals of the chandelier. The hanging prisms twisted and touched each other, making a light, brittle sound that filled the great hall. Al-Awkary was truly in a sweat, as he saw inner meanings unfolding around him.

He directed Tess up the stairs to the second floor and then to the fourth door to the left of the staircase. Tess counted the steps up the staircase, and the doors between her lock-up to her freedom. Her prison cell was a large, beautifully furnished bedroom. As she scanned the room with Al-Awkary, she never changed her facial expression. Her eyes came back to rest on Al-Awkary. Tess saw a visible chill run through him again. He pointed toward a door that was half ajar. Tess was sure it was the bathroom. They stood facing one another, and no words passed between them. Al-Awkary walked out the door, and Tess heard a dead bolt slide into place.

Tess urgently needed to go to the bathroom. She didn't know if she was being watched, but if you have to go, you gotta go. The bathroom had large mirrors covering all the available wall space. Her reflection was drawn and pale, and she felt the tension easing as she seated herself on the toilet.

She wasn't sure how to handle the experience of being kidnapped. It felt good to be alone to think. She scanned the bathroom for surveillance cameras. She still had her long coat around her and noticed how cold it was. It was probably below zero outside. The morning weather report said there would be a warm-up over the next few days. She wished she could be at home, shoveling snow on the walk, doing normal things. Her hardest chore would be better than playing whatever game she had been dropped into. As scared as she was for herself, she was more afraid for Jack. Tess was sure he would come for her. Suddenly she remembered her phone. She yanked it out of her pocket and almost cried when she saw that it was dead.

Tess washed her hands, splashed cold water on her face, and walked back into the bedroom. She went to the large, curtain-covered windows and pulled back the heavy, blue silk drapes. The windows were covered on the outside with thick metal bars. Light from large, street-sized lamp posts spaced about every twenty feet along the snow-covered garden path lit up the scene below. The snow and wind had stopped, and a large full moon shone brightly from above.

Tess took a slow, deep breath to hide her excitement when she realized that she knew this place. Tess had visited her friend Casey many times in their youth in this beautiful home. The large barn and horse fence in front of her looked the same as it had twenty-five years ago. She and Casey had ridden together to train for the Olympics—which seemed to be a lifetime ago.

Casey had married a Canadian and moved to Quebec about the same time Tess and Jack married. The family home was now being rented out for large corporate parties, and to foreign dignitaries who had extended business stays in the US.

Tess talked to Casey a few years ago, after Casey's father passed away. Casey's mother and brother had been killed in the 9/11 terrorist attacks at the World Trade Center. Casey moved the family business from New York City to Canada. She was keeping the family estate until she could let the memories go. Casey would not like her home being rented to terrorists.

Tess knew the back entrances to the kitchen and family room. She knew everything about the barn and stables and surrounding woods. She was sure nothing had changed after the death of Casey's mother. She had been the horse lover of the family.

Tess took a blanket from the big bed, sat in a comfortable wingback chair with a matching ottoman, and wrapped the blanket snugly around herself. She couldn't make herself remove her shoes. She wanted to be able to run for freedom if she was given half a chance.

She was almost warm when the hall door opened. A woman entered with a tray of food without making eye contact or speaking. Tess didn't move from her cocoon. The woman placed the tray of tea and soup on the table beside the chair Tess was wrapped up in.

Without a word, the woman turned and left the room. The sound of the deadbolt sliding into place made Tess cry.

What an odd slice of time, Tess thought. Here she was—locked up in her friend's home, not knowing why she had been kidnapped, and being served food late at night by a Middle Eastern woman. She was probably racially profiling, but they didn't seem to be from the neighborhood.

Tess smelled the good, strong tea and hot, spicy soup. There was even pita bread with olive oil. She hadn't realized how hungry she was. She took a sip from the hot mug of tea and started on the soup. The spongy bread was delicious dipped into the thick soup broth. Tess was looking into the bottom of the bowl when sleep overcame her. Her last thought was, *I've been drugged.*

It was the next day about noon before Tess came around from whatever she had been given. The sun was shining through the big window that Tess had pulled the drape back from the night before. She sat up suddenly when she realized where she was. Her head did the nauseated pound and spin from the drug. She was in the big bed, all covered up. Someone had moved her from the chair to the bed. To her relief, she was still fully clothed. She wondered why they had drugged her.

The sound of the sliding bolt and door opening made Tess jump, and her stomach did a spin. In walked Al-Awkary and the woman from last night.

Al-Awkary asked, "How are you feeling this morning?" Without waiting for an answer, he said, "You know nothing. You have to get up. We will be taking you home shortly. We are exchanging you for your husband." The woman placed a bottle of aspirin and a cup of strong, black coffee on the table by the bed. Without another word, they both turned and walked out.

Tess climbed out from under the covers and stood up. Her stomach did a flip, and she ran to the bathroom and threw up. Whatever they had drugged her with last night had given her an all-over body ache. She decided to take four of the tablets and hoped they were really aspirin.

The hot, strong coffee helped clear her head and settle her stomach. Tess stepped over to the window to look out over the snow-covered garden. She saw the two men from the van and Al-Awkary standing in a tight circle, talking and smoking their skinny black cigarettes.

Al-Awkary must have felt her eyes on him. He suddenly turned and looked up at her window. She stepped back out of sight and watched as they dropped their cigarettes and mashed them into the melting snow. She was still feeling shaky and dizzy from the drug they had given her. Her fear of death at the hands of these foreigners was overwhelming her. She wanted to go home and be with her family.

The sun was melting the snow from last night's storm. It was falling off the roof in big, wet chunks and dripping water off the house, trees, and anywhere else it had stuck during the snowy blast. It had to be about forty degrees for the snow to be disappearing so fast. It was a beautiful Central New York day for October.

It was not Al-Awkary who came to take her home. Tess had not seen this man before. He stood solemnly in the doorway of her room and stared at her for a moment. He motioned for her to come. She was sitting on the ottoman at the foot of the big chair and was slow in responding to him. Before she could fully stand up, he came over and yanked her to her feet. He slapped Tess hard across the face, losing his hold on her arm. Tess tumbled backward over the ottoman and hit her head on the end of the solid mahogany footboard of the antique bed. She was out.

Tess came to in the back of the van. She was lying on her side in the cargo area, and her face and head were throbbing. She started gagging from the taste of blood in her mouth and tried to sit up, but the back van seat was pushed as far to the rear as it would go. It had her pinned tightly against the back doors.

Tess started crying. She thought about her parents and the terror they had gone through at the hands of the thugs who killed them in their Florida home. These might be the same men. First anger and then rage filled her. She would get even. Tess wasn't feeling like a victim anymore. She felt the need to hurt these vicious bullies that had hurt her and her family. And she would.

Tess could tell by the light coming through the van windows above her that it had to be late afternoon. The van had veered to the right off the thruway when they came through the EZ-Pass lane without needing to stop to pay an attendant, then turned left at the highway. Tess couldn't believe it, but it seemed they were really taking her home. She hoped they wouldn't kill her and leave her body for Sara to find. She decided she would come out fighting.

The van slowed to a crawl and stopped. Tess heard the driver's door open but not close. She figured he would shoot her, dump her, and then drive off. The back hatch had a flip-out window that had to be opened first, and then the bottom half doors could be pulled opened.

Jubi Asnad Sutwan had made a deadly mistake in hitting Tess. Al-Awkary was so angry that Jubi was lucky to get by with just a vicious beating. He was sure at least two of his ribs were broken. His left eye was swollen shut, and his nose was broken and would not stop bleeding. Al-Awkary told him that his fate was still undecided.

Jubi Asnad decided to put the Tess out at her house and drive on to New York City. He had friends and family there. They were all happy in America, and he thought he could be too. He was deep into his own thoughts when he opened the van doors to drag the woman out. He was not prepared for the tiger that pounced on him.

Tess had felt around under the seat of the van for anything to use as a weapon. Her hand closed over the tire iron lying by the jack. When the doors opened, she came out swinging. Tess hit Jubi Sutwan so hard on his right temple that he was out for the count.

C H A P T E R

5

Sara stood at the window and watched the road for any sign of her mother. Her father had called her about two hours ago and said Tess would be home shortly.

An agent by the name of Thomas White was waiting with Sara when a van slowed up and stopped at the end of the driveway. They both watched with their mouths open in amazement as the driver opened the back of the van and Tess leaped out and hit the man on the head with what appeared to be a tire iron.

Sara and Agent White ran out the kitchen door and down the driveway to Tess. She was standing over the unconscious man with the pipe still in her hand. Sara grabbed her shaking mother and hugged her. Tess dropped the tire iron to the ground, and mother and daughter burst into tears of relief as they held each other tightly.

Agent White put the unconscious man into the cargo area of the van that Tess just came out of. But Agent White took the time to tie Jubi Assad's hands behind his back with plastic handcuff strips that had been left lying on the floor of the van. This kidnapper would think twice before leaving an American woman free to fight back. Thomas called for assistance in taking in the lone kidnapper suspect.

Tess and Sara climbed into the van, and Thomas drove them to the house. Sara filled her mother in on what her dad told her—that Tess had been exchanged for Jack.

Tess jumped out of the van when they got to the house. She ran into the kitchen and pulled a holstered gun and ammunition out of the back of the bottom cupboard.

Sara kept repeating: "Mom, Mom, what are you doing? Let me help you."

Tess said to Sara: "Hook the truck up to the horse trailer, saddle two of the mares and Raven, load them in the trailer, and pull up to the kitchen door. I'm going upstairs to change my clothes."

Tess ran up the stairs and into the bathroom where she turned the shower on hot and strong, stripped off her clothes, and stepped under the steaming water. She soaped from head to toe in less than two minutes, toweled off, and ran naked across the hall to her bedroom.

Agent White had just reached the top of the stairs to check on Tess as she came sprinting from the bathroom and across the hall, slamming her bedroom door behind her. She pulled on cotton long johns, her favorite jeans, and a heavy black turtleneck sweater. Thick socks and boots came next. Tess rubbed her medium-length hair as dry as she could and pulled a sock hat over her damp brown curls. She glanced at her reflection in the mirror and saw strength and purpose in her eyes. The purple bruise that covered the right side of her face filled her with fear for what they would do to her Jack. She was sure they would show him no mercy.

Agent White didn't know how to get control of this situation. It looked as if the mission was already under way. He heard a loud knocking at the kitchen door and ran back down the stairs to intercept an intrusion by a friend or neighbor because everyone knows the enemy does not knock. It is an agent he has worked with before.

Becky Lindsey was standing in the kitchen door that no one had taken the time to close. Becky had driven all night and day to get to Central New York after dropping off a delivery of weaponry to a silo north of Atlanta, Georgia. Becky had been alerted that help was needed by a brief message from Jack. Later, a call came from her headquarters to drop everything and get to the scene of the situation pronto.

Becky got many phone calls with updates on Tess's situation while on her trip to make a weapons delivery. She had made the long drive down busy Interstate 81, leaving her home in Alexander, Virginia, at five o'clock the previous morning so she could arrive near Atlanta, Georgia, around ten that night. She drove her 450 Ford Dually, which could easily pull her six-horse trailer with its hidden cargo. Her two Tennessee-gated show mules made the trip with her, loaded in the first and last stalls. The middle four stalls were loaded with missile- tracking devices and special equipment for satellite hook-ups. There were also eight wooden crates of AK-47 automatic machine guns and ammo. Hay bales had been stacked on top of the crates to hide the load. What could be seen through the windows of the trailer were the mules' big heads and the large, fresh hay bales. The mules and hay were the cover for this heavy delivery.

Becky didn't have to explain the weight at the interstate weighing stations. The kind state employees just flagged her around all the big trucks. It was a very heavy load, but the large diesel engine of the made-to-work truck didn't even seem to notice. Becky had the cruise control set at sixty-seven miles per hour, so as not to attract the interest of the state troopers. What's more American than a farm girl traveling with her horses? She looked the part with her long, brown hair pulled back in a ponytail. Her saucer-sized, deep blue eyes gave her a girl-next-door look. But her serene stare went deep and could search the soul of anyone or anything she found worth studying. She was tall at five feet seven inches. Her workouts were cleaning the horse stalls and helping at her brother's crop and beef cattle farm.

Agent Becky Lindsey was an FBI weapons specialist. She had been assigned the job of arranging the deliveries of weapons to prepared farm silos from Virginia all the way through Georgia to Florida.

After she took the time to walk, feed, and water her mules at the delivery site, Becky loaded the road-weary jennies back into the trailer and headed for home. She was traveling much faster without the heavy load of weapons. Becky had called her brother, so he was there to take care of her tired pets.

Becky ran into her cozy log cabin, grabbed a soda, and took a ten-minute hot shower. After throwing a few things into a travel bag, she was out the door. She jumped into her black Ford Mustang and took off to help in the recovery of Tess. Meanwhile, Becky's laptop gave her updates on Tess's kidnapping as information came in.

The thugs who took her were dedicated to the take-down of America. The locations of the weapons hideouts would be helpful to them in the guerrilla warfare that would be happening soon if the leaders of America didn't get their acts together.

This woman, Tess, was just a fly in the ointment of a huge production. The moving of equipment, weapons, and securing safe places to store them was a critical safety net for the people of the United States. If war happened, everything had to be in place.

Becky stood in the open doorway of what looked like the entrance to the kitchen, wondering what was going on. A fellow agent she recognized came running down the stairs with a frustrated look on his handsome face. Right behind him came an even faster-moving Tess.

Becky had been receiving downloads to her computer of pictures of those involved and as much detail about the situation as was available. She saw things had changed. Becky couldn't miss Tess's battered face, but there seemed to be no damage to the rest of her body.

Tess was armed and heading for the door. Agent White was trying to slow her down, but Tess looked to Becky like a woman with determination and, most likely, a good plan.

Sara, just back from the barn, pushed past Becky as if she wasn't there. "Mom, the horses are in the trailer. Everything is done. I'm ready," she said.

Agent White made a quick introduction of Becky.

As they all stood just inside the kitchen door, Tess explained her plan of action to save Jack. She walked to the refrigerator to grab a soda and to the cabinet to pull out a box of crackers. To the agents she said: "Go to the bathroom and get what you want from the kitchen. Be at the truck in five minutes, or be left behind."

They all did a quick scramble and loaded up for the mission.

Tess climbed into the driver's seat of the Ford 350 Dually. The large truck had a little age, but didn't have a payment.

Young Sara rode shotgun. Agents White and Lindsey climbed into the back seat and had to push horse blankets and two bags of feed to the floor. Tess had picked up the horse and chicken feed at the feed store on Saturday and never unloaded it into the barn feed room.

Lights from a car coming toward them up the driveway lit up their path. Agent White let his window down and shouted at the man jumping out of his car. "The prisoner is in the back of the van. Stay at the house with him until you are told differently."

Tess came to a rolling stop at the end of the drive. Seeing her small posse, she said, "I just want to thank you in advance. This is going to work. We will save Jack."

C H A P T E R

6

Al-Awkary had never thought much about death. He had always been too busy fighting his way through life. But now he was afraid. He had seen his spirit's shadow come and slam to the earth in Tess's eyes. His end was near.

There was no moon this night. The brittle glow of thin, white light from the bulb that hung from the high ceiling of the horse stall shone down on the battered body of Jack. Al-Awkary and his men had been brutal in their treatment of their prisoner. Al-Awkary had just taken his sharp knife and cut a deep circle around Jack's neck to show him where his head would be cut from his body if he didn't tell them where and how weapons were being hidden in America.

Jack would never tell.

Al-Awkary was not happy with the way this mission had gone. He was angry with himself about Tess being knocked out, and couldn't understand why it made him so crazy. So he took out his frustrations on Jack and almost killed him. He told his men to stop with the punches. They turned Jack loose, and he slumped to the stall floor in a bloody heap.

Al-Awkary and his men locked the heavy wooden horse stall door with the flip of the latch. Jack couldn't open it from inside the stall even if he could get his battered body to stand up. The three men go to the house to warm up and have a snack. Beating up an

American gave them a good feeling. It came in a close second to killing one.

Tess knew the back drive into the barn area. It was heavily wooded and not visible from the house. She backed the truck and horse trailer just deeply enough down the dark, tree-lined driveway entrance so as not to be visible to traffic coming down the unlit, narrow country road. The four rescuers, now American militiamen, silently got out of the truck. Becky and Sara climbed into the trailer to keep the horses quiet and to wait for Tess's call. Agent White and Tess started the long hike to the house to find where they were holding Jack. The bridle path Tess loved to ride in her youth was still clear enough for her and Agent White to do a half-slumped, fast walk toward the back of the large house. The dim light coming from the tall outside lamp posts softly lit up the back gardens. The light kept them on track as to their location relative to the house and barn. The thin light was just enough to keep their shadowy figures blending into the trees and thick bushes.

After about ten minutes of walking and half crawling through the thick woods, they finally came close enough to the back of the house and barn buildings to get a visual of the area. Just when Tess was deciding on their next move, out of the barn came three dark figures. The glow of their cigarettes made it easy to follow their progress through the snow-covered gardens to the back entrance of the house. There was no small talk—not a word was said between the three men as they walked toward the warmth of the house. Tess disliked their heavy silence. It filled her with fear for Jack. But seeing the three men come from the barn let her know where to look for him.

Agent White put his hand on Tess's arm as she started forward, but she turned and gave him a look that burned into him. He knew he had to follow Tess without questioning her.

Tess had explained her plan to Sara, Becky, and Thomas on the drive over. Everyone had accepted the part they were to play in the rescue.

Tess and Agent White would locate where they were keeping Jack. When they needed backup, they would call Agent Lindsey.

Sara would stay with the truck and horses. She had a rifle her dad had given her for her thirteenth birthday, and she would not hesitate to use it to protect her family.

Tess and Agent White crept around the big barn and went in through the back entrance. Two lights glowed dimly about twenty stalls toward the front entrance. That was where the thugs had come from. Tess and Agent White hugged the dark walls and crept silently toward the only spots that were lit in the huge, old barn. No horses were kept here anymore. All the feed buckets and horse brushes were in their places, waiting for the owners that would never return.

Jack had to be in the first stall, just before the barn manager's office. The half-open office door made a semicircle of light that shone toward the main front entrance. The huge sliding doors on the front were pushed tightly shut.

Tess prayed that Jack would be in the barn, not the house. Agent White looked in each stall on the right-hand side of the barn. Tess looked on the left. Her frightened heart shooting up into her throat was the only thing that stopped the scream from coming out of her mouth.

Jack was on his back as if he were dead, lying on the hard, cold, clay floor of the first stall. Tess unlatched the lock, slid the heavy door open, and ran to Jack. He stirred as she softly called his name and rubbed his cold hands. When Tess saw how battered and bloody Jack was, she wanted to kill his assailants. Agent White entered the stall, but stood at the stall door, so he could keep his eyes on the entrance of the barn, his gun in his hand and ready.

Tess was almost cooing to Jack as large tears spilled down her face. Agent White was afraid Tess has lost it, but then realized she was already rattling off instructions to Sara on her cell phone. Sara and Becky were to ride the two mares and lead the stallion up the delivery truck driveway entrance to the back door of the barn. Tess would get on Zane, and the others would get Jack up to her. The stallion was the only horse Tess had that wouldn't spook at the sight and smell of blood. She was sure she could trust him to stay calm with Jack in this condition and get him back to the truck. The girls were already on their way. Now Tess and Agent White had to get poor Jack out of the barn fast.

Jack's spirit had been floating above his battered and bleeding body. His eyes felt as if they had sunk so deeply into his brain that he was seeing with his mind's eye. He saw a soft, flickering glow like a campfire. It appeared to be on a hilltop a quarter of a mile away. He saw figures around that light, some sitting and some standing. They seemed to be waving their arms in a motion that told him to come and join them. Jack felt their warm, loving spirit in the joy of seeing him. A soft, cool breeze twirled around him, pulling him forward, as if to gently help him on his last earthly journey.

All at once, a flash of Jack's earthly love yanked him back. He thought—*Tess*. Then he heard her voice—her soft, loving voice that she always used when talking to their children. He had always cherished hearing the sound of the love-filled words.

Jack was so thirsty. The blood from his beating had filled his mouth and clung to his teeth. He was exhausted. Hearing Jess's voice had to be a dream. Jack had exchanged himself for her life. Tess couldn't be here in harm's way—but she was. Jack felt her hand holding his. He even smelled her sweet, clean breath on his face. He saw the waving figures at the campfire, but now they were signaling for him to go back to Tess. His spirit rejoined his body with a hard thud that made him jerk awake. The pain that shot through him was overwhelming, but worth it to hear his Tess cooing to him. He would never leave her again.

Tess saw Jack take a deep breath that shook his whole body. It brought him back to the living. His face was so badly swollen from the beating that he could open his eyes only into narrow slits. Tess was aware that moving Jack in this painful condition would be dangerous, but they had no other choice.

When Tess and Agent White stood Jack up between them, they realized he would have to be carried. Tess silently thanked God that Thomas was big enough to do the job. Thomas gently lifted the battered warrior. Tess would have to be the backup, but she was ready to shoot any of these men without hesitation. She just hoped she would be a good enough marksman to make the bullet count.

The threesome hurried down the dark barn hallway to the back door. Everything was quiet except for Jack's raspy breathing.

Tess realized that she had been holding her breath. She took a deep gulp of old barn air. A flashback of happy memories of her and Casey's fun times filled her with renewed strength. Life is what you are willing to put into it. America, Jack, her children, and friends—Tess would win this battle over evil for all of them, but first there would be more fights coming. She just had to fight them one battle at a time.

When they reached the back entrance, Tess stepped up to unlatch and push the old, heavy barn door open with her gun ready. The lights from the house and garden glowed faintly, turning the outside world of trees and underbrush around them into thin, weaving shadows of light and dark. They started to retrace their steps down the old, brittle path to the truck when they heard Sara and Becky whisper a greeting. The two were waiting for them with the horses at the edge of the trees. Sara and Becky stepped forward to help. Thomas told Tess to get on the horse, and that he would pass Jack up to her. Becky and Sara helped support Jack as Thomas lifted him up in front of Tess. Jack gripped the huge black horse's thick mane and leaned heavily against Tess. Sara and Becky got up on their horses, Thomas jumped up behind Becky, and they started the short journey back to safety.

The horses did a fast walk back down the drive to the truck and trailer. Jack could not have taken much more jogging. Everyone had their guns ready for any sound or movement from the house or barn, but all stayed quiet. Jack was carefully loaded into the back seat of the truck, with Tess on one side and Sara on the other. It had taken eighteen minutes to get this mission done. Becky loaded the horses into the trailer and jumped into the driver's seat. Thomas was ready for trouble, with his gun in position.

As they pulled out of their hiding place, they heard shouting and gunshots. Becky stepped on the gas as the glare of flashlights came weaving through the woods toward them. Shots rang out, but they were already on the road and out of harm's way.

Tess had no other plan of action. She just wanted to take Jack to the nearest hospital.

But Jack had other plans. He was coming around, and his mind was working overtime. He looked at Tess and said, "Give me four aspirin and a long drink of that Coke. I'll be okay."

Thomas said, "What do we do now? We'll be easy to pick out on the thruway. The thugs will catch up to us shortly."

Becky was driving as fast as she dared. The roads were clear of snow, and they had already made it to the turn for the thruway.

Jack looked at Tess and said, "Head for home."

Becky and Thomas were wondering what happened to Al-Awkary and his men. Tess and Sara were just looking at Jack.

At that moment, a large black car pulled up beside them. They all watched as the passenger window rolled down and a friendly American face, known to Agent White, looked back at them. Thomas had called for backup before they arrived at the barn. What they saw was it. The black car moved over in front to escort them home, and another dark car pulled in behind the horse trailer. It felt good to be watched over.

Home never looked so good. They must have left every light on when they rushed out to rescue Jack. Like a beacon in the night, every window seemed to be standing at attention, welcoming its family home.

As they pulled in the driveway, an unmarked police car was leaving with Jubi Sutwan. He wouldn't make it to New York City. With today's laws, he'd probably be deported to his home country. There would be a no reentrance visa for America, and a red alert to other countries. He would be tagged!

A doctor was waiting to check Jack and Tess over. The medical team was at the house with a full medical emergency unit, complete with X-ray machine.

Tess wouldn't turn Jack's hand loose. She climbed into the medical truck as the men carried the stretcher holding Jack. Jack's shoulder had to be put back into place, and two of his ribs were cracked from the kicks he received. He was hurting, bruised, swollen all over, and would have to be watched carefully for days. He needed stitches on the nasty cut around his neck.

When the doctors finished their treatments and checks, the soldiers carried Jack on the stretcher upstairs to the big bed he and Tess had shared for what seemed a lifetime. The doctors would come twice a day to check Jack over, and Tess would not leave his side.

Jack looked into Tess's eyes and told her, "I never thought I would be in this bed again. I have always loved you, and I thought I was keeping you safe. I should have told you everything."

Tess replied, "Yes, you should have. You are here with me now, and I know the danger, but not the reason. So tell me."

Jack asked everyone to leave the room. Then he briefed Tess as he would have told any fellow soldier on his team. He left nothing out.

Tess excused herself from the team of medics, who came back into the bedroom to finish hooking up the IVs and getting Jack as comfortable as he could be in his battered condition. She went into the bathroom and had a five-minute cry. She washed her face and looked in the full-length mirror at herself. Her face would take a little time to heal. She was glad she hadn't lost any teeth from the hard slap to her face. The knot on the back of her head was throbbing, so she took two aspirin from the bottle on the counter, and drank a full glass of water. As she turned to leave the bathroom, Tess caught the true reflection of who she is in the full-length mirror on the back of the bathroom door. She saw a good, strong American patriot, one willing to fight for her family and country's safety. She gave herself a salute.

Tess returned to Jack and their bedroom. The fact that it was once again the two of them in the same bed sounded wonderful to her. It filled her with happiness.

A male army nurse with a large gun had made himself comfortable in Tess's overstuffed reading chair in the corner. Sara was sitting on the floor by Jack. She was holding his hand and talking about taking her driver's test soon and about the Jeep she sort of wants.

Agent White was waiting for Tess at the foot of the bed. He said: "Tess, Al-Awkary and his men are still out there. They aren't quitters, so we know where they will come at some point in the near future. Their mission is to find out Jack's mission, and we can't let that happen. Some of the soldiers, including me, will stake out your farm for now. We will have to find Al-Awkary if you are ever to be safe. We feel Jack is safer here than in a hospital. We will give him around-the- clock care as long as he needs it. We will send you and Sara away for a while. You need a safe spot with people to protect you."

It took Tess only a moment to think this through. It was obvious that Jack was the bait the army was going to use to catch the bad guys. She said, "Sara and I will not leave Jack."

Thomas looked at the loving family, who were so glad to be together again, and said, "I would not have expected less." He said good night to them, and went downstairs to report their decision.

Sara stood up, kissed Jack, walked over to an exhausted Tess, and gave her a gentle hug. "I'm so proud to be your daughter," she says. "I love you both. See you in the morning."

Tess climbed into the bed slowly so as not to hurt Jack. She moved over closer and put her knees gently up against him. Jack's hand found hers.

Their guard moved quietly about the room, tuning out the ceiling and bedside lights, then settled himself back into the comfortable, oversized leather chair with the perfect reading lamp. Both items had belonged to Tess's dad. He chose a book from the pile of novels and magazines Tess had collected all summer to read on long, cold winter days and nights. Tess and Jack were asleep before their protector turned the first page.

Tess awoke with pillows tucked against her where Jack should have been. He was an early riser, she a sleep-in snuggler. Jack's pillow trick had always worked like a charm and let her get another hour or so of sleep.

Tess smelled bacon frying. She couldn't believe Jack was recovered enough to cook breakfast. One of the medics had come in during the night and unhooked Jack's IV after checking him over. Tess grabbed her jeans and a favorite old, soft sweatshirt and headed for the bathroom. She gently brushed her teeth in her sore mouth and took a hot shower. Her aching and bruised body started to relax under the hot, steamy water, and she came out of her bath feeling content and safe, confident they could handle whatever life threw at them as long as they were together. Tess rubbed her curly, damp hair dry and pulled on her comfy clothes and slippers. She needed some of that hot coffee and that great-smelling bacon. It was way past time for barn chores.

As Tess stepped down the stairs, the sound of Jack's soft chuckle filled her with happiness. There he was, sitting in his chair in their cozy den. Everyone was listening to one of the young soldiers telling some tale. Another soldier in camouflage was frying up the bacon. Sara was sitting on the floor, leaning against Jack's chair with Jack's hand on her shoulder. It made a happy, almost party-like scene. It brought to Tess's mind the saying "the quiet before the storm."

Agent Becky came in and announced: "The barn chores are done. So where is breakfast?"

Tess stepped up to the counter and filled a waiting mug with fresh, hot coffee. The baby-faced soldier, who seemed to be in charge of cooking, handed her a plate of food with a quiet "Ma'am" and a slight nod of his head. Tess went over to sit on the arm of Jack's chair, and his arm slipped around her waist. As she ate her breakfast, sipped her coffee, and listened to the happy chatter around her, she sensed the quiet peace they all needed for mental and physical recovery to ready themselves for the battle to come. Tess felt the undercurrent of alertness from each of these warriors and was proud that she and Sara had joined their ranks.

When Agent Thomas's phone rang, he stepped through the arched doorway leading into the formal living room of the old house. All the camaraderie stopped in anticipation of what Thomas was hearing. After a few long minutes, Thomas stepped back into the kitchen and found all eyes on him as he shared the news.

"I will repeat the message I just received from the agent in charge of finding the kidnappers. They evacuated the big house where Jack and Tess were held and then vanished. They left their clothing and food cooking on the stove. They must have just run out of the house and driven off after Tess snatched Jack out of the barn.

"The agents are widening the circle of their search. The airports in Rochester, Syracuse, and Buffalo are being watched, and the Canadian border crossings have been alerted. We know they still want Jack because he has the answers to their questions. But they will not get Jack. Tess will see to that!"

There was a cheer and a clinking together of coffee mugs in a salute to Tess.

Al-K couldn't understand how everything went so wrong. He kept playing and replaying it around in his head like a broken record playing the same tune. His thoughts tortured his days. If he fell asleep, he awoke suddenly, and the same theme of "what ifs" twisted around in his head.

He didn't feel well, either. His head hurt and his stomach felt heavy and uncomfortable all the time. He wanted to go home. For the first time in his life, he didn't feel safe. The two men that had been with him from the start of this mission were uncooperative and whispered between themselves. When Al-K came into the room, he heard hard, angry talk going on between them. It was not the words, but the heavy intensity of suppressed emotion between the two that worried him. They would go silent when he came near them. Their intense looks felt like knife stabs in his back as he walked past. He knew he was walking a dangerous line with them. They both carried guns.

Al-K had lost their respect when he protected Tess. They felt he should have killed her instead of turning her loose and had been angry ever since. He now felt the same way. Al-K would kill Tess. That was the only way he would ever get peace again.

The three gunmen were close to Jack and Tess's home. They had an apartment in Baldwinsville, New York, about twenty minutes east of it by back roads or thruway.

Al-K wanted to go home and warm up. He wanted to feel the hot, dry heat of his homeland. He dreamed of lying on his house's rooftop with one of his wives and being hot all over, body and mind.

The weather was cold tonight, as it always seemed to be in Central New York, but at least there was no snow. The skies were bright and clear, and a full moon would shine tonight.

They had been waiting almost five months to bring this to an end. It was time for Al-K to act. This mission would be over with the killing of Jack and his family. Al-K was finished with trying to get information. It was done.

It had been almost five months since Tess was kidnapped from the college parking lot. Tess, Jack, and Sara had dropped back into their regular routine. Agent White and Agent Lindsey returned to their regular assignments about a week and a half ago. The two young Army guards stayed to help Jack with the gun deliveries for now because of his injuries.

Jamie and Tom were coming home from college for Easter break. They were delighted that their mom and dad were back together. They would be told everything that had happened while they had been away at college. They couldn't stay safe if they didn't know the danger hanging over their family's heads.

Tess was in the barn, her favorite place to relax. She was sitting curled up in a large high-backed rocking chair with an overstuffed seat cushion. Her father had made two of these chairs for barn seating. It was a great place for a friendly chat or to discuss any problem that came up.

It was the first week of April and a beautiful New York day. The sky was crisp, clear, and blue. Days like this gave the promise of the warmth to come in the months ahead. There was still snow under the shadows of the big spruces trees. Tess was sitting deep enough inside the doorway of the barn to be out of the wind. The sun's rays poured in the door and warmed her body and her memories.

Tess strongly felt the need to see her sons. The touch—the connection of the human spirit between a loving parent and child—was a wonderful thing. It was also full of responsibility. Tess had never been separated from her boys this long. They had always been loving and supportive to her, as she was to them. Watching them grow up had been a wonderful, fun time. The house had always been full of family and friends. They had weekend campouts and cookouts. There was plenty of food and snacks. Boys were always hungry. Jamie and Tom loved the horses and the farm. When the two were young, they told both parents at different times that they were never leaving home. Then time passed, the twins grew up, and life called. Tess did hope they would one day settle near her.

The boys were driving Tess's old black Tahoe SUV. The big car was built like a tank and looked like one. They were dropping off a couple of friends at their homes on the way. Everybody chipped in to help pay the fuel on the long drive home. The high price of heating and car fuel was taking a chunk out of everyone's pocket.

The boys knew where to find their mom this time of day. They parked at the house and went straight to the barn. The smell of their mom's cooking was drifting out the open window of the kitchen. It mixed with the clean, spicy odor of the huge blue spruces that were waving around in the wind as if to greet them. These were just a few things that made this wonderful spot home.

They went in the back door of the barn so they could sneak up on Tess, as they had since childhood. Tess was in deep thought and did not hear them come in. Tom reached out and touched her on the shoulder. They didn't expect her to jump out of her chair like a bullet and look as if she was ready for battle. Tess recovered quickly and gave each son a bear hug and they all had a laugh. They finished the barn chores together and started walking to the house.

Jack drove up from another gun delivery with the two young soldiers riding along. Jamie and Tom could feel a difference in their family—an undercurrent of alert watchfulness that had never been there before.

Jack greeted his sons with a papa bear hug and then a handshake. He introduced them to the soldiers, who were not much older than Jamie and Tom. They all went into the house for a late lunch. Sara would be home from school shortly, and then they would fill the boys in on the dangers the family was up against.

It was a good thing because Al-K and his men would be coming sooner than they thought.

Al-K checked his handgun again. He didn't understand why he was so jumpy. His men were not nervous as far as he could tell. They looked as if it was just another evening out to dinner. The apartment they were sharing was much nicer than the spaces they usually rented. In America, all the material things were better than in any other country. The food was wonderful and always available. You couldn't drive a mile through the many towns and cities without finding a fast food or a fine dining restaurant, and many were open around the clock. There was so much luxury here. Al-K would miss the amazing food the big shower that never ran out of hot water in the apartment.

Their plane reservations were already made for the next morning. They would drive to JFK International Airport outside of New York City, and their plane would leave at 7:45 a.m. This mission would be over with the killing of the family.

Al-K and his men had staked out Jack's home. They knew the family would be settled in by nine thirty this evening. Al-K wanted them dead by midnight at the latest. The weather was getting nasty. The wind had been picking up steadily, and it had started spitting a little snow. The temperature must have dropped ten degrees in the last couple of hours.

Al-K hated the cold. His joints had started giving him trouble. His back had a pain that would come and go, but when it came, it would shoot down his leg. He blamed all of the problems he was having on Tess. He was going to be the one to kill her; he owed it to himself.

10

They had a great day planned. The whole family had gotten up early and gone car shopping for Sara. She had been given her parents' permission to skip school for this happy occasion. They covered four dealerships by lunch and still hadn't found the perfect "Sara car." Either the price was too high, or the color was wrong. They were all having fun. It was an important milestone in Sara's life to find her first car.

At lunch, the family had all agreed to make one more stop before giving up the search for that perfect buy. Home was calling to them. The boys and Sara wanted to ride the horses over to the silos to see the fancy revamping to the structures. Jack had to be at the silos for a drop-off of equipment that he would be delivering this week into the Thousand Island area of New York. He needed his sons' help with some of the loading and unloading of the heavy crates.

They stopped at a small family-owned dealership, and behold: there sat Sara's dream Jeep. It was a bright, lime green with a black retractable roof. She went straight to it. The interior had light brown leather. The little beauty even had heated seats.

Jack and Tess could tell this would be the one if the price, mileage, and information were right. The Jeep had a good, one-owner history, so the deal was struck. Sara would take it home for an overnight trial run. Jack wanted the Jeep checked out by his mechanic. If everything was OK, it was Sara's. The brothers were ready to share their driving expertise with their inexperienced baby sister. It was a memory that Jack and Tess would always keep close to their hearts. The thought came to both of them as they reached for each other's hand that being together and sharing family milestones was a precious thing. As their eyes met, the strength of their love and commitment to each other, their children, and their country was like the sun's warm glow shining around them. They could feel God's blessings on them. Being together again was a loving kiss from heaven.

The kids drove straight home and then went straight to the barn to start saddling the horses. As Tess and Jack drove up, the kids called out to their parents that they would be at the silos in about forty-five minutes. Jack left Tess at home with a kiss. She would do her usual chores and get started on supper.

For Sara and her brothers, the weather was just right for a long ride. The temperature had dropped into the fifties. The water in the stream was moving fast from snow melt. But if you and your horse knew where to cross, it was only a foot or so deep. The threesome had been playing in and around this creek all their lives. The horses knew the safe crossings better then their people. All the livestock would cross over for the fresh grazing on the other side of the stream. You could head the horses into the direction of the stream, give them their head, and say, "Move on." The horses would carefully pick the point to enter the water for their best footing.

The boys and Sara made it across the stream and entered the deep forest on the other side. Jack had cleared a twelve-foot path so they could use it for horses, snowmobiles, or trucks. They used the trail to check on their livestock daily.

Tess had stood and watched the happy trio jog off. The mellow smells and sounds of barn, horses, and her family clung to the air and warmed her heart.

There was a misty haze in the sky to the east. Tess hadn't watched the weather reports for a few days. She needed to check and see what was coming their way.

As Tess turned and walked to the house, she realized the dogs had gone for the family adventure with the kids. She would have to remember to put them in the dog yard tonight. It would be a few hours before her family came back. As she walked into the kitchen, she looked at the time. It was already three o'clock, but this time of year, the days stayed light until about seven. She had plenty of time for a cup of tea. There were seasoned hamburger patties in the fridge, ready for the grill. Tess had picked up potato salad and slaw from one of her family's favorite delis, The Original Dill Pickle. So dinner was ready when they were.

The army was exchanging the soldiers who had been guarding them for two new men. They would not be coming until the next morning. Jamie and Tom would be heading back to school in the morning, too, and the family would get back into its normal routine.

Tess suddenly realized this was the first time she had been alone since her kidnapping. A chill went up her spine, and it felt like the hair on the back of her neck was standing up. She was sitting in Jack's favorite chair in the den, and everything around her was silent. But it wasn't a peaceful silence. It felt like the calm before the storm.

At that moment, the old tea kettle let out its shrill whistle, and Tess jumped straight out of Jack's chair. "Chill out," she said out loud to herself as she walked over to the stove and added her tea bag to her favorite cup and poured the steaming water over it. She moved over to the kitchen window and looked down the long drive from the house to where it met the road. A slow-moving dark van was passing by the end of her drive. The strange van acted as if it was going to turn into the lane to the house. But then it just crept on down the highway.

Absolute fear filled Tess. She slammed her mug of tea on the counter, picked up her car keys without slowing down, and ran out of the house to her car. She was stiff with fear. Just as she opened the car door, the dogs came running up to her. Their funny, smiling dog faces, with their long tongues hanging out from their run, brought her back to reality. She could breathe again. She hadn't even realized she was holding her breath. Tess inhaled a deep, lung-filling breath of sweet air and thanked her dog friends for bringing her back from fear. They walked back into the house together. Tess was glad no one had seen her so freaked out with panic.

11

Al-K and his men had driven by Jack's house earlier in the afternoon. There were several cars in the drive, not ones that they had seen there before. Al-K hoped there were not overnight guests to have to deal with. Maybe when Al-K and his men came back, some of the people would be gone. If not, too bad for them. They drove around a bit and decided to stop for soup and a sandwich at the Old Erie Restaurant in the middle of the small Erie Canal town of Weedsport, New York. They were now just about eight miles south of Jack's house. Everyone in the restaurant noticed the three men with heavy accents and Eastern looks, but of course no one would say anything because that would be racial profiling and wasn't polite.

The three were enjoying their food and talking about being home in just twenty-four hours. They were so glad this mission was as good as over. They were talking in their language and didn't even consider that some stupid American might be able to understand them.

One of the young waitresses, Jayla, was a student at Cayuga Community College in Auburn, one of Tess's students. She had heard about the kidnapping of Tess, who was everyone's favorite teacher at the College. Jayla was not in her class the previous semester, when the incident happened, so Jayla had only heard the hearsay. The happenings had gone hush-hush. No one seem to know what really happened.

Jayla knew firsthand about being terrorized. She had escaped Iraq and was granted political asylum in the United States. A family in Weedsport, New York, had sponsored her. This was a kind, accepting place to recover from the murders of her family and friends in her home country. She was waiting on the table next to the three men and had her back turned toward them. Jayla heard remarks that made her take a step backward to get a little closer to their table so as to hear the men better.

Jayla felt fear grip her all over. It was like a large, greasy hand clamping its fingers around her heart. She had heard that voice in her past. She had been away from her country six years, but she would never forget that voice.

Al-K had come to her small town three times, the first time to murder all of the men of the village. He had taken her grandfather and father with all the men in the village they could capture, lined them up in the street, and shot them all.

About two weeks later, Jayla and her older sister Ruby were behind the house, hanging up the hand-washed laundry on the clothesline, when screams and then gunshots rang out. This time Al-K and his thugs murdered her mother and grandmother. The sisters hid all day. They had nowhere to go and no help would come to them. The village had been tagged for death. The other villages were afraid to help. They knew it would bring the wrath and retaliation of Al-K to their village if they interfered with his torture of these poor souls.

The third time, Al-K and his men came in the middle of the night. Al-K took Jayla's sister Ruby, who was just fourteen, and gave her to one of his men. Jayla never saw her wonderful sister again.

Jayla was thrown into a dark, filthy prison cell with ten other children. Somehow she stayed alive in that horrible place for nine months, three days, and twelve hours. American soldiers freed Jayla and the other six children that had survived through the Ayatollah's cruelties. The children had all been shipped to America, hopefully to get their health back after the starvation, and to try to recover their minds from the mental terror.

Jayla had found peace in Weedsport. America was now her home.

She realized she couldn't stand in the middle of the busy restaurant for more than a moment without being noticed. Her feet felt as if they were glued to the floor from her fear. Jayla had to move and move fast. The table she was waiting on was celebrating their grandmother's eighty-sixth birthday—a family of six happy, never tortured, lucky Americans with lots of love and safety surrounding them. Only Jayla was aware that one of the most hated and brutal devils of Iraq was seated at the table ten feet away.

Al-K felt an icy tingle run through him. It was the feeling of death. Something or someone had reached from the grave and put fingers around his heart. It lasted only a moment. If the chill had lasted longer, he would have been dead.

His men were talking to him comfortably. They were so happy to be going home that they had not noticed his momentary pain. Al-K was seated in a large, high-backed chair in the middle of the room. The restaurant was full this evening. The food was excellent. He had gained weight from the wonderful American food he had grown to enjoy. The service was also very good. His waiter had filled his water glass several times without his asking. Most of the servers were women. He never even bothered to look at them. Women were good for only two things: sex and hard work. No woman was any better or more special than any other. A woman could easily be replaced.

Jayla walked to the kitchen and went straight to the back door that led to the parking lot. She called over her shoulder to one of the cooks, "I need some fresh air. I'll be right back in." She stepped out into a beautiful spring evening. The sky was a deepening dark purple and blue. The sun was almost done for the day, just a little rosy pink glow on the edges of the trees. Jayla dropped her head and prayed to God in heaven to give her the strength and direction as to what her line of action should be.

The soft, cool breeze lifted her raven black hair and fluffed it into a cloud around her beautiful face. She was a small, delicate beauty. Her large, bright, almond-shaped eyes were full of too much knowledge of the hardships of a cruel world.

She decided that the thing to do was to go back into the restaurant and continue listening to the conversation of the three men. Jayla would then follow the men to their car and get the license plate number. She would call the state police as soon as the thugs were away from the restaurant. Jayla would not bring harm to her friends here or at her American home. She had lost everything once. She would not allow it to happen a second time.

Jayla took the dinner bill to the birthday group's table and boxed up their take-home food. She smiled and laughed with the family, but heard everything that was said at the table behind her with the three Iranians. They were now talking loudly in Arabic. Jayla had not heard it spoken in many years. All of her family and connections with that life had been murdered.

The birthday family went out the door, so Jayla could listen as she cleared their table. The men were talking in loud voices, confident that no one could understand them. Jayla heard Al-K telling the other two men that he was going to kill the woman, that neither one of them could touch her. If they did, he would kill them both.

There was a dead silence. One of the men coughed nervously a couple of times. The other one cleared his throat. Then they started talking about the first thing they were going to do when they got home on Tuesday evening.

Jayla pushed the dish cart back to the kitchen. She told the head chef that she would have to run home. "It's a girl thing," she told him. "I will be back in twenty minutes." Jayla didn't wait for an answer.

She ran out into the parking lot. Because she had walked to work, she had no car to hide in. Four large garbage dumpsters lined the back end of the deep, dark, narrow parking lot. She hid behind the first dumpster. There was a pathway behind it that led to a back street and freedom if the men spotted her.

She didn't have long to wait. Two of the men came out the side door of the restaurant and started walking straight toward her. She silently slipped a little deeper behind the large, smelly dumpster. They were close enough for her to hear their words of anger and resentment toward Al-K. He had pushed them over the edge with his threats. The words were coming so fast that Jayla was having a hard time understanding, but she knew the gist of their meanings. One of the men said, "Let's kill him here and throw him into the dumpster, where he truly belongs."

The other man thought about it for a moment and then whispered: "No, we will need his help in killing the family. We will shoot him after we finish the mission. That way, we don't have to explain what happened to Al-K. The men that hired us know Al-K is too old for this type of mission. We will tell them he became careless."

The two men unlocked the van, backed out of the parking spot, and sat with the engine running at the side door of the restaurant, waiting for Al-K. His dinner had not agreed with him. It was probably the dessert of rich chocolate pecan pie with heavy whipped cream.

Jayla had her waitress pad and pen. She stepped out from behind the dumpster just far enough to see the license plate number and the make of the van. It was a dark blue 250 Ford passenger van in with one taillight out. She watched as the man that had taken everything from her in a different life drove away. She ran out to the street to see the direction they were heading. Jayla watched as the taillight disappeared into the darkening night. Then she took her cell phone and calmly dialed 911.

Terrorism in New York State is a touchy subject. The 911 operator listened to Jayla once, asked a few questions, and then turned her over to his boss for more questioning.

Elizabeth Thompson was a retired FBI agent. She was at the end of her service to her country. She had purchased a two-hundred-year-old farmhouse with lots of acreage and the usual two-story, huge red barn that she planned to fill with horses. It was located on the banks of the Seneca River. The small town this young woman was calling from was where Elizabeth did her grocery shopping and banking. Her office was at the thruway building at exit 40, about two miles from the restaurant. The van must have been passing near her office right then. Elizabeth sent a car to pick up Jayla so she could question her personally.

Elizabeth called headquarters to check on any terrorist activity going on in the area. The name and address of one of her neighbors immediately came up on the computer screen as a high-profile protection case. She scanned the info and got a 99 percent feeling of where the thugs were heading. This was definitely a code red.

C H A P T E R

12

Tess, Jack, and the family were full of good food and the fun of the day. They rented a scary movie from cable for the night, a science fiction war movie. Tess didn't think she would be able to sleep after watching all the wicked cruelty toward mankind.

All that evil was what they needed protection from. They didn't need to be choosing it for entertainment. Tess looked at her wonderful healthy family and did a once-over of her warm, comfortable family room. She want to imagine being invaded by foreign forces from anywhere in the world, much less from another universe.

Tess had been wondering what had happened to Al-K and his men. Maybe they got out of the country. It had been almost five months since her kidnapping. In some ways it had worked out to be a blessing for her. Tess didn't know if she ever would have had her family back together if Jack had not had to save her from Al-K.

Their separation and divorce made her a different person. Tess learned to stand up for herself and knew how far she would let herself be pushed. Tess and Jack were on a level playing field now. She would never accept her life as just an extension of being a caregiver for a man and children again. Tess now saw her time on earth as being as important to mankind, her family, and America, as any other warrior fighting for freedom.

The government was always pushing people not to "leave a footprint on the earth." To Tess, that was wrong. The issue wasn't the footprint, but rather the type of footprint to leave. We all need to work hard to make a difference in the short time we have here. We are responsible for improving everything around us for the next generation. Until we see ourselves as precious, wonderful creations, we will never see the amazing people our children and grandchildren can become. Tess could never sit back again and let life just happen. She would be a fighter mentally and physically.

Tonight was to be one of those testing times.

The twins were night owls. They were born into the world at two in the morning. It happened on a snowy night in February, nineteen years ago. Their internal time clock from that moment on had been set for late night studies or partying until the sun came up. They were not sleepers but doers.

The plan had been to leave early in the morning to go back to school. The twins decided to wash clothes and pack the night before. The last load of jeans was doing the flip-flopping tumble in the dryer.

The two young men were not just twins, they were best friends. They always had each other's backs. Jamie and Tom both planned to be attorneys and have a practice together in New York City. They wanted to go into politics in the most powerful city in the world.

But on this night, their parents and sister were in mortal danger. They looked at one another and knew they couldn't leave until this danger was over, so they decided to take the semester off. One of them would travel with dad, and the other would stay with Sara and mom.

The brothers stepped outside to talk. The sky was spotted with fast-moving, white, cottony clouds. The moonshine spilled down through the trees like floating silver. Everything around the young men seemed to be moving in the ever-changing, shimmering moonglow. The changing play of light and shadowed darkness made it hard to see anything clearly.

Tom and Jamie's home had always been a safe place. They intended to keep it that way. No outsider would come and destroy their family's way of life. They would stand guard tonight and every night as needed. And they wouldn't leave until Mom, Dad, and Sara were safe.

Al-K and his men pulled up a dirt lane that the farm tractors used to get to the fields beside Tess's barn. A strip of hardwood trees and large pines grew between the lane and the barn. The men felt safe hiding their car there for a quick exit when they were through with their mission.

It was hard for the men to walk very fast because of the play of the light from the moon and clouds shining on, around, and through the trees. Before they adjusted to the dark, the clouds moved, and the silver glimmer poured down on them from the moon again. It was difficult to know where to take the next step. If someone happened to be looking their way, their shadowy movements would be easy to see. It was impossible to stay hidden in the bright moonlight. Time seemed to be waiting for this final play of action to begin.

The night was still, and there was a biting chill to the late evening air. It was just the right sleeping weather for New Yorkers, with no sound of humming air conditioners, no chatty TV or radio, and no passing cars at this time of night. It looked like all good Americans were home, reading a good book or sleeping.

Al-K and his men didn't know that Tom and Jamie wee home. They didn't know that the army guards weren't back yet. So they thought this would be an easy kill.

Sara couldn't sleep. The moon shone brightly through her large bedroom windows, and the glow lit up her whole room. She held her hands up in the air to see how the moonglow looks on the skin of her arms and hands. She was so excited about her new Jeep. It was exactly what she dreamed of for her first car. She couldn't wait to drive it to school and show it to all of her friends. Sara hopped out of bed and went to the bedroom window to see if she could catch a glimpse of her new Jeep in the driveway. She had parked it next to her mom's car near the kitchen door.

Sara's bedroom was on the second floor, looking out over the barn and the woods beyond. She loved her view through the big double windows. Her grandfather built the window seat under the window, and her grandmother made the beautiful, soft pillow cushions. They had a bright wildflower fabric in her favorite colors.

Sara started to tear up at the thought of her wonderful grandparents being murdered just a short time ago. Why would anyone want to kill such loving people? She missed their bi-weekly phone calls and would never get to visit them in Florida again. She had always stayed with them for a month every summer her whole life. Sara wondered if the people who tried to kill her parents were the same ones who had murdered her grandparents.

Her windows looked out on the north side of the house. Sara was always the first to spot the changing color of the trees or the coming of the first snowfall. She loved this house, and knew how blessed she was to have such a wonderful family.

Sara was sitting all covered up on the window seat and looking out at the world when her brothers walked outside. One leaned against his car, and the other stood straight and tall, with his hands in his pockets. Sara couldn't make out what they were saying. She heard only the muffled sounds of their voices floating up to her. Sara's windows were closed against the cool night. She guessed it had to be about eleven o'clock. Her brothers had always been night owls. She wished she understood what they were saying, so grabbed her robe to slip out and join them.

As she turned to reach for her robe, the clouds drifted away from the face of the moon. A movement between the woods and barn caught her eye. Her heart skipped several beats as she counted one … two … and then three figures carefully emerging from the line of trees. They were spaced out maybe twenty feet apart and walking with their heads bent as if that could hide them from the moon's bright shine. She had to warn her brothers. The men would be on them in minutes. Sara grabbed her rifle that she had kept hidden by the head of her bed since her mother's kidnapping.

Sara ran silently down the stairs and out the open kitchen door, which her brothers had left open while they loaded their car. Sara slipped up to them so quickly that Jamie jumped and exclaimed: "Jesus, Sara!" She put her finger to her lips and pointed her gun toward the barn. The two young men came to attention.

Sara told them that three men were coming toward them from the back side of the barn. "Get in the house and lock the doors. I'm going back up the stairs to tell Mom and Dad."

The three moved back into the house. The only light came from the laundry room's half-closed door. It spilled out into the hallway to the kitchen and den. Tom flipped the light off and then found the loaded shotgun that hung on deer antlers over the door. Jamie retrieved the loaded Remington rifle from the den. The soldiers took the bigger weapons with them. Now the brothers stood with guns pointed at the ceiling, waiting for instructions from Jack and Tess.

Sara ran back up the stairs to her parents' room. The door was open, and she started whispering to them as soon as she entered the room.

Tess and Jack woke up instantly. Sara told them what was happening.

Jack slipped on his jeans that were on the floor by the bed, stepped into his moccasins, and got his handgun out of the drawer in the night stand, all seemingly in one quick move.

Tess pulled her favorite sweater over her nightgown, got her handgun and cell phone out of the stand on her side of the bed, and slipped her feet into her slippers. Both Tess and Jack were ready to get this over with.

Sara told them where the boys were. She started for the stairs behind her swiftly moving parents but then decided to run back to her room to see if she could spot any figures from her window. She opened the window and listened. One of the horses whinnied, alerting the dogs, now in full howling mode. The big stallion pranced full throttle out of his stall from the barn and into the fenced paddock. The big horse started snorting deeply and charged at a figure Sara saw crouched by the fence. Sara spotted another man with a gun in his hand and a large pack on his back. This man walked toward the front of the house.

By this point, it had been about seven minutes since Sara spotted the figures coming out of the trees. She ran back to the stairs to tell her family what she had seen. Jack and Tess had just gotten down the stairs and to their sons. As Sara started down the stairs to join her family, a lime green dot appeared on the wall just to the right of her head.

Jack screamed, "Get down now!" Sara dropped down flat on the stairs, as the bullet passed just over the right side of her beautiful, young face. It hit one of the framed photos of the family and blew a fist-sized hole in the pale blue wall.

Tess screamed and Sara shouted back, "I'm fine," as she bumped down the last two stairs and crawled behind Jack's big chair.

Jack, Tess, and the brothers came to life. Tess ran to Sara, and they put their backs against the wall, with the big, thick chair in front of them. Tess called 911 on her cell phone as the gunplay began.

The fast-moving clouds slid away from the bright moon, and the house filled with silvery light. Tess had always loved her floor-to-ceiling windows and no drapes. They made you feel like you're part of the outside. But now it was making it easier for Al-K and his gunmen to see the inside of the house like a lit up stage.

Al-K guessed Tess would be hovering over the girl. He couldn't believe his shot had missed her. It had been such a clear shot. He would not miss again.

Tess dropped the phone on the chair and pushed it between the cushions. When Tess didn't speak to 911, they would trace the call and send troopers out to check what was happening. She didn't want the light from the phone to give their hiding spot away.

Al-K and his men were wearing night vision goggles. They weren't much bigger than most sunglasses, and they let the killers see right into the den. Al-K saw the toe of a shoe sticking out from behind and to the right side of the kitchen island. He pointed his powerful gun up two feet from the toe of the shoe and to the inside of the cabinet twelve inches and pulled the trigger. Half the cabinet blew apart, and the front of the refrigerator exploded, with milk, soda, and food flying everywhere. It had only been Tess's shoe, which she had slipped off her tired feet after the family's fun day.

Tess took this opportunity to crawl out from behind the chair. She pulled shaking Sara by the hand, and they ran out the back door, calling to Jack and the boys to run. The men agreed that getting out of the house was the best plan of action. It was like being on stage, with the moonlight coming so brightly through the big windows.

Tess thought "bomb" about the same time the idea came to Jack. These men wanted them dead, and a bomb would erase their family and home instantly. They didn't want to be trapped inside the house by running upstairs, so the only thing to do was head for the barn and woods.

Al-K couldn't believe his man had not covered the back door. He didn't know what happened to him. The plan had been for Al-K to line up the kills through the downstairs windows. His two men would get anyone who came out the front door or back door. Someone from the family must have spotted them. Jack and Tess had somehow known that Al-K and his men were outside, but only by a matter of seconds. Al-K was angry with himself for missing the girl. Being such a close family, they would have all run to help her. If he had gotten her with that first shot, he could have killed all of them. Now he didn't know where Jack and Tess were or where his men disappeared to.

Tess told Sara in a whisper, "Run for the barn!" She hoped Jack and the boys would follow them. When they ran past the dog pen, Tess remembered that the dogs were out. The guns back there were too much for her little handgun to stand up to. They would have to win by wit and cunning, not weapons.

Tess and Sara stopped at the big tree in front of the barn. Its thick, wide branches hid them for a moment to look back for Jack and her sons. Tess saw by the way the figures moving toward her that it was her beloved family. She stepped out from the tree and they saw her. The family grabbed each other and hugged tightly for a moment.

Al-K stepped around to the front of the house and right into his man. They both cursed and then praised Allah that they had not shot one another.

Neither one knew where the third man was.

The dogs knew. The stallion had alerted the dogs to the approaching stranger. Tess had forgotten to take the dogs back to their pen before she went to bed, and the boys had left the kitchen door open, so the dogs went out the open door of the house and to the dog pen to get into their big dog house with their favorite blankets inside. The assassin that was supposed to guard the back door of the house had climbed through the pasture fence and came creeping past the horses. The stallion chased the stranger out of his corral and straight in front of the dog pen. The two 175-pound girls came barreling out of their house and chased the thug back through the woods and into the van. The dogs paced around the van, jumping at the driver's window. Their vicious snarls and bared teeth convinced the foreigner that it was time to go. He happened to be the driver and had the keys. The other men were not his family. He has\d his plane ticket in his pocket, so he was leaving. The others could take a car from the house they were blowing up. He had stayed in this crazy country long enough.

So he backed the car down the dirt lane to the road and turned toward the thruway. He drove about two miles before a state trooper came flying by with his lights and siren wailing. He had made the right decision. Al-K would be caught or killed, and he would be safe from Al-K's retaliation for giving up on the mission.

He made it another mile before he noticed flashing headlights coming up hard and fast behind him. The van was not built to outrun a New York State Police trooper, but this weary Afghan tried. The Seneca River was deep and very wide, and the current swift. The van was going at its top speed of 125 miles an hour when the edge of the front bumper touched the side of the bridge. It flipped over three times and went sufficiently airborne to flip over the railing and down into the dark water. It was probably a kinder death then Al-K would have given him if they had ever met again after this botched mission.

Tess, Jack, and the rest of the family headed for the forest and fields behind the house. That would be a safe haven from the guns. Two four-wheelers were waiting for them behind the barn. The boys would drive, and Tess and Sara climbed into the seat behind them. Jack whispered, "Start and go now." He was going to bridle the stallion and follow them to the silos. The engines kicked into gear, and the four took off into the night. Jack held his breath, praying he wouldn't hear gunshots. Unbelievably, there were none.

Jack stopped for a moment to think. At that moment police cars came flying up the drive with lights flashing and sirens wailing. The headlights of the troopers' car caught Al-K and his man heading toward the woods after Tess. Al-K ran down the hill and into the woods. His gunman held back until Al-K disappeared into the night before putting his hands over his head and walking slowly back to the troopers. They handcuffed him and put him into Elizabeth Thompson's unmarked FBI car. It would be her last arrest before retiring.

Jack's family was far ahead of Al-K, so Jack knew he had a moment to tell the troopers what was happening. He needed a bomb squad to check out the house. Al-K and his man had spent too much time at the front of the family's home not to have done something that would destroy it.

Jack briefed the troopers and sent two squad cars down the highway to be there when Tess and the kids arrived at the silos. Then he put a bridle on Zane but didn't take time for a saddle. He took the horse over to the fence, climbed to the top rail, and jumped on the big horse's back. Zane was keyed up from all the strangers and confusion in the middle of the night. Jack wrapped his hands into the long, thick mane to hang on through a few hard bucks from the excited horse. Then they took off after Al-K.

Three state troopers were walking through the woods with flashlights, and a helicopter was flying overhead with large searchlights blazing on a scene of running deer and confused birds seeking a safe place to hide.

Al-K was furious and unable to believe what was happening to this mission. His men were gone, and he had no clue what happened to them. He needed help with this failed mission. He was all alone, wading through waist-deep, icy water, chasing after fast-moving three- wheelers. What was he thinking? He had a flashback of seeing his spirit crash to the earth in Tess's eyes. He had seen his fate. Why did he stay when he believed his life would end here on Tess's land? This would be his last battle, but Al-K would take Tess with him to the afterlife.

Al-K made it to the other side of the stream. The four-wheelers were fighting to get up the steep hill and over the crest. He took his rifle and tried to aim from where he stood, but he was too far away.

He ran into the clearing where he had seen the headlights of the ATVs enter the trail. The clouds had cleared from the sky and the moon was shining with a frosty brightness. It seemed to be directly over his head. The strong, cold wind was blowing the branches of the tall trees, making a constantly changing pattern on the ground with their shadows. Al-K had a hard time knowing where to put his feet. The play of light and dark made the ground an undulating trail of unseen rocks with dips and holes to slow his progress from the chase.

A startled deer came tearing out of the bushes and almost ran him over. Because Al-K's finger was on the trigger of his powerful rifle, he shot into the rocky ledge right in front of him. A shower of dirt and gravel rained down on him, filling his face and eyes with dirt and grit.

He hated America. Only here could a wild animal make such a stupid thing happen to him.

As the four-wheelers topped the hill and flew through the freshly plowed field, the grinding of their motors added to his feeling of having no hope of ending this mission successfully.

He made his way to the top of the hill, his heart pounding and his legs aching from the climb. Al-K saw three lonely farm silos on the far side of the huge empty field. They were tall, with blinking lights on the top and sides so airplanes would not fly into them. He wondered why the group was heading toward these buildings. The glare from the headlights of the four-wheelers lit up the lower third of the first silo. The lights were turned off and all went dark. The silence was eerie after the loud grinding noise of the ATVs. He heard the clink of a metal gate closing and the rattle of a lock snapping shut.

Al-K felt totally isolated from his world. Why had he fought this battle so hard against Jack? He was one of the only people Al-K ever admired. Terrorist wars were directed by greedy Hitler types, causing chaos for innocent people, everyday people just trying to live, work, and protect their families and homes.

The men he represented were extremists and terrorists. Why had he let them rule his life and put him here to kill or be killed? He was truly a man without a country, a man who had never been kind to anyone. He had never been loved or protected since he left prep school, and he had never given love or protection to anyone. Al-K had killed thousands of men, women, and children. He had killed them with knives, guns, and bombs. He could look them in the eye and kill them or shoot them in the back. It had never mattered to him before. At least until now.

Al-K walked through the field toward the woman who made him think about life's "what-ifs" for the first time in his fifty-two years on earth.

Why had he been so bitter at life and mankind? He was so young when his parents were killed he couldn't even remember them. He never appreciated the people who saved him. He never gave the healing the kind family offered a chance. He had seen many starving and dying people and never gave them a second glance. He had been alone all his life by choice. Al-K had only cautious, murderous acquaintances and women who had been given to him as rewards for his terrorism as his companions. Tess was the first person to make him question his life.

He had been cleaned up and placed in that prep school many years ago to meet people that would come to occupy powerful positions in the world. Why had it not changed him? He wouldn't let these mistakes continue.

Jack heard the shot of Al-K's rifle. He was so afraid for his family that tears rolled down his face without his even knowing it. The fear that gripped his heart was terrifying. As Jack and the big stallion topped the hill, he caught a glimpse of a shadowy figure leaving the field. It had to be Al-K. In another few minutes, Al-K would find his way over the fence surrounding the silos.

Jack kicked Zane in the sides with his bare heels. He had lost his slippers in his wild run from the house to the barn. Zane couldn't run in the wet, muddy field. He was sinking up to his knees in an uneven jumping jog across the wide-open expanse. If Al-K had looked back at the moonlit field, he could have picked Jack off the big horse in one easy shot. But it didn't happen.

Jack rode the gasping horse up to the chain-link fence and leaped to the fence in his panic to get into the compound as fast as possible. He had to stop whatever Al-K planned to do to his family. Jack climbed up and dropped over the fence to the muddy ground and sat on his heels to listen for any movement. The wind was blowing harder, and a misty rain swirled around him. The loud metal ping of harder rain was hitting the tops of the silos, muffling any sounds of human movement nearby.

Jack prayed that Tess and the kids would stay locked up in the silo. He didn't think Al-K could get through the locked steel door.

He ran over to the first silo and stood against it, then worked his way around it until he was standing in the middle of the three silos. Jack heard his Jeep's engine start up with a roar. He had left it in the barn at the back of the third silo with the keys in the ignition. It came to life from a heavy foot on the gas pedal.

Jack heard the state troopers' sirens and saw the flashing lights coming down the side road. It was twelve miles by highway from the house to the silos. Because of the rain, it has taken the troopers longer than Jack by horse.

The Jeep backed out of the low barn with a squeal and flew past a startled Jack, smashing through the chain-link gate and heading straight for the oncoming police cars.

The first police car swerved out into the field to avoid a crash with the Jeep, but the next police car wasn't so lucky: the Jeep hit it head on.

Al-K had not buckled up. The twelve-year-old Jeep hit the seven-year-old patrol car and did an end-over-end flip. Al-K was flung out of the Jeep and flipped seven somersaults through the muddy field. He broke an arm and a leg in the first few flips, but it was the broken neck that finally ends this murderer's life. He died looking up at the ink-black sky. The silver shine of the moon coming through the rain mist lit the scene in front of Jack. He ran over to Al-K in time to hear the last word the man would ever speak. Ad ham Al-Awkary whispered: "Tess."

Tess, Sara, and the boys rushed out of the silo when they heard the horrible, screeching crash of metal on metal. Ambulances with flashing lights and sirens blasting pulled up to the scene as the family reunited by group hugs.

This American family would never understand the man who tried so hard to kill them or the way he ended his life of brutality toward mankind.

Jack looked at the faces of the Americans standing around the broken man breathing his last breath on earth. Tess slid up to Jack, and he wrapped his arms tightly around her. They were all sad that a life ended in such a painful and brutal way, regardless of what he had done.

The paramedics worked diligently to stabilize him. The police were ready to help his man in any way they could. Everyone stood around the broken body of Al-K as his life ended on American soil. Jack and his fellow Americans bowed their heads in prayer for Al-K's soul. Jack added, "Thank you, God, for making me and my family Americans."

The family were then driven home by New York's finest.

Sondra's by the Sea

Preface

This short story will always be one of my favorites. It woke me up at midnight after a particularly hard day at my shop. The story line kept playing in my head till I was fully awake. I went to the kitchen so I would not wake Robert and where I always keep a notebook and pen at the ready. I worked for over three hours before Robert came to the kitchen to check on me. I still could not stop with the writing and correcting of each paragraph. I worked literally till the sun came up.

My stories fill me with a different world of people and places. They seem to become real in the space of time that I work with the lives of the characters, their families, and their adventures. They call me to my favorite keyboard. And it is there that their lives begin.

Hope you enjoy "Sondra's by the Sea." Thanks for reading.

—Sheila

Sondra's by the Sea

Sondra's by the Sea is a favorite seafood restaurant of the locals and beach vacationers to the area. It has been a hopping place today. Thursdays are normally slow and easy with morning walkers and paper readers. Sondra, the owner, head chef, and bottle washer, has not even had time to place an order by phone to the fish market for tomorrow's early morning delivery. She will have to pick it up herself. There is nothing like the smell of raw fish, black coffee, and fishermen at five in the morning to wake you up and start your day.

Today her restaurant is full of business types. Three-piece suits aren't her usual clientele. The barefoot beach strollers are the normal morning and lunch crowd. Sondra enjoys mingling with her customers and hearing about their lives. Politics is always an invigorating conversation starter.

Sondra has come from the kitchen to the dining room for a check on the waiters and hostess.

A nervous thirtyish man had been waiting at the bar for his party to arrive. The three men he is waiting impatiently for enter the restaurant just as Sondra walks up to the front. Sondra picks up the menus from the busy hostess and shows the four to their table in a corner. The nervous man had requested the back corner spot.

Sondra takes their drink order and feels guilty about racially profiling the three slick-looking Middle Eastern men. She wonders why they would be meeting with this loser. There are several briefcases in tow. It has to be some kind of business meeting. They give her a bad feeling. But hey—she had been home only a few months from her marine duties in Iraq. Detonating bombs for months in a hostile foreign land would make anyone a little suspicious of foreign accents.

Sondra wanders among the tables and visits with the townsfolk and the beach visitors. About the time she thinks everything is winding down and the crowd is thinning out, two cars pull up to the front restaurant entrance, and eight large men in suits and dark glasses walk in and scan the dining room. They are the wrestling team from Auburn University of Auburn, Alabama. They have come to Gulf Shores for an awards presentation and a weekend of sun, sand, and girl chasing.

Time stops.

Three of the four men at the back table, who had been deep in conversation, stand up and carefully watch the men who have just come in. Sondra can see that they are on full alert. An electric wave of emotion weaves its way through the restaurant. It feels like the hot desert wind she had felt blow past her in the arid lands of Iraq. Sondra knows from the way they stand that these men are carrying guns. The loser probably has one, too.

The three foreigners walk out of the restaurant, get into their car, and drive off. In an instant the danger is over. The loser is left sitting at the table alone. He slowly stands to leave. In one quick motion that he hopes no one sees, he pushes the item he was showing the men between the large potted tree and the wall that is next to their table. He drops money on the table so a waiter won't chase him for the tab and tip and then walks out of the restaurant.

The loser doesn't stop until he is about two miles down the beach. He waits to see if anyone follows him. No one does. He goes into a beach bar for a beer and a think.

The group of happy young college athletes at Sondra's remove their coats and order beers and raw oysters fresh from the Gulf. They will never know how close they had come to being gunned down.

Sondra goes to the phone and describes what she thinks is an event with bad guys. Her friend at the troopers' office listens to her and says he will do some checking into it.

Sondra wonders if anyone else had felt the dangerous chill of the moment. Then a call for help comes from the kitchen and her mind shifts to other things.

Seth—the loser—has his car parked in the public beach parking lot. He has to move it before sunset or it will be locked in the lot till morning.

He is not good at this. Being a thief is hard work. Seth had spent three years in prison for stealing auto part designs from a Toyota factory. Toyota had hired him from a youth outreach training program in the late nineties. When he got out of prison, Uncle Sam paid his college for engineering, paid his housing, and supplied him with a spending allowance. It was a great gig. All the pretty young girls loved Seth's tale of taking the wrong path. They took him home to Daddy's house for Thanksgivings and Christmases. Seth stole cash and jewelry at each visit. No one ever pressed charges. They were too embarrassed that their daughters had turned a fox loose in their homes.

Seth doesn't see the need or have the staying power for a college degree. He couldn't make the grades because he wouldn't do the work. He's a loser who wants to be a big-time thief, and Uncle Sam is helping him get his dream.

The dream is called Pensacola Naval Base in Pensacola, Florida, where Seth got a job as an assistant to a research team. He is working in a program for the misguided and unappreciated, paid for by American tax dollars. A short time ago he would not have passed clearance, but the new administration has changed the rules. Seth gets his chance and goes for it.

Seth is the type of person no one notices. His light brown hair is cut short, his face shaved clean, he uses no cologne, and his dress is always earth tones. He is five feet eight inches in height and about twenty pounds overweight. He doesn't stand out in a crowd.

That is his plan, and it works.

It is mid-morning on a hot August Monday. Seth walks into a secret conference that bigwigs from the US, Belgium, the UK, Switzerland, Finland, and Germany are attending at the base for the week.

The dark room and intense information exchange make it easy for Seth to fade into a back corner chair and get comfortable. In display that is lit from above are seven devices in a row. Country of origin and information sheets are in front and behind each device. The decision- makers can easily read the maker from anywhere around the table and take the fact sheet to study at their leisure.

Four of the devices are similar in their rectangular shape and typical black and steel gray color. Three to seven buttons and indicator lights do not make one stand out over the other to Seth. The other three are different.

Switzerland has two entries on the table. One is round, with a steel gray face and a deep purple band of glow-in-the-dark super plastic that holds the device together. It is about ten inches in diameter and has all the lights and buttons anyone could want. There other entry is baby blue, square, and comes with all the bells and whistles of mass destruction.

But it is the strange little one that Seth cannot take his eyes off of. It's Finland's entry, an octangular box, gold-plated over steel, with sterling silver trim. The lighting on the device turns a hot amber color as the delegate from Belgium picks it up. A soft warning beep lets him know that this might be a mistake, and he gently puts it back on its stand.

This is the one Seth will take. The people who are paying Seth an impressive million to steal it don't care which one he brings them.

They will get billions of dollars worth of research from any of the seven detonators.

Seth stays at his desk looking busy until after six on Wednesday afternoon. The base is throwing a big seafood dinner for the already overweight delegates. Many state politicians and high-ranking military officers are coming. Most of the security personnel have moved over to the dinner site. They will give their protection and receive a wonderful free meal of fresh seafood from the Gulf of Mexico.

Seth hides in a stall in the men's room till six thirty. He comes out to an empty, peopleless hallway. He walks past empty offices till he comes to the door of the conference room. He holds his breath as he turns the doorknob. All kinds of excuses go through his head to explain why he would still be in the building and trying to enter a high security area. He waits for an alarm to go off.

All is quiet!

Seth enters, goes to the device of his choice, and drops it into the paper bag he used for his lunch. The device does not like Seth's lunch bag. It starts its soft beep and begins to glow. Seth is too busy to notice. He rearranges the other devices so it isn't quite so obvious that they are now one short. He walks back to his office and places the blinking and beeping device into a foam box. Seth slips out the side door to a fenced area used for smokes and bagged lunches. It has concrete picnic tables and no shade. A chill runs up his back. This spot has always reminded him of prison.

He tosses the box over the fence and behind some ragged boxwood bushes that are suffering from the Florida heat and government neglect, then goes back into the building and walks down the office corridor for the last time and out into the parking lot. His car is parked as close to the bushes as possible. Seth still has to walk down the sidewalk to nowhere, which is used only by the maintenance man or trash pickup. The video surveillance camera will probably catch him in the act of retrieving the box from behind the bushes. He just hopes he is far, far away by the time they start putting two and two together.

Seth goes to his apartment to pick up his small packed suitcase and drives to Pensacola where he spends the night at an airport hotel. He ditches his worn-out Toyota and rents a new car to make the deal. After he has the money in his hands, he will drive to New Orleans for a few days of fun. The world will be his oyster!

The delegates will not be back in the conference room till Thursday at one in the afternoon. It is now about ten in the morning, and Seth is driving west on I-10 to the Robertsdale and Gulf Shores exit. He has chosen a beachside restaurant by the name of Sondra's by the Sea. He had seen the owner's *Channel 3 News* interview on the continued effect of the oil spill cleanup on area business. Seth feels patriotic spending his money to help a small business owner in trouble. He will buy lunch as a celebration for himself after his meeting.

There is no traffic on this Thursday morning at the beach. As Seth drives into the center of the small town of Gulf Shores, the mid-morning sun is glittering off the amazing azure blue waters of the Gulf of Mexico. The sea gulls are squawking with glee, but the incredible sound of the waves and smell of it all never touch his soul.

The restaurant is easy to find, and Seth is early. It is almost eleven, and the connection he had made from his Moslem acquaintances during his prison time, will be at Sondra's by noon. He goes half a block down the street to beach parking and walks back to the restaurant. It is now eleven-forty, and he feels that his life is starting to take a turn—and it is!

After the disaster of the lunch meeting, Seth moved his car to the restaurant parking lot next to the dumpster. It is after ten at night, and the surf is not only pounding on the beach behind him, it feels as if it is pounding in his head. He had wandered into the sun porch of the restaurant around seven that evening to glance in the corner, looking for the detonator. It was still there! He had jammed it far back into the crevice between the wall and the flower pot. Luckily, the orange and red flowers that overgrew the pot and spilled down its sides are distorting the soft blinking of the object. He starts toward it just as three state troopers come in the front entrance and ask for Sondra. A young and helpful waitress notices him standing there, out of place, and asks how she can be of help. He hands her a dollar and without a word walks out.

By now security will surely know the device is missing at Pensacola Naval Base. There will be panic first, and then bulldog determination will drive the hunt for the missing object.

It won't be long before they look in his direction. The surveillance cameras will tell the tale.

Seth can visualize it: all the important people coming into the conference room after their morning of sunny beach and good food. They would have happily greeted each other with slaps on the back and small talk. Someone would have noticed that seven devices had become six. Finland would scan the table for their device and scan it again. Then the uproar would begin. There would have been shock and anger from Finland and a security lockdown of the base. The clock is ticking and the hunt begins!

The Yemenis had called to set up another meeting for the buy. Seth lied and told them that he had the object. They are to meet at midnight at the closed entrance to the public beach parking. There is enough room to pull in side by side on the two-lane entrance. Seth plans to get there first so he can back his car in for a quick exit after the deal is struck.

Seth is tired of this game. He has watched the employees come out of the restaurant by ones and twos. Now it is just he and Sondra.

Sondra loves her spot in life. Great food and the Gulf of Mexico go hand in hand. It is her place now, and she is the fourth generation to hold onto this little spot of land and a great business. Through hurricanes and now oil spills, she and her family have survived.

She is also a weekend warrior, proud to be a marine.

Sondra flips the switches to lower the lighting and steps out to the front entrance of the dining patio and into the glow of a quarter moon. The sound of the Gulf's surf playing its water tune on sand makes her want a cool late-night swim. As she makes a final scan of the front of the restaurant, a soft amber blink stops her in her tracks. Since she served time in Iraq as a bomb specialist, the blinking light sends the hairs all over her body straight up.

Sondra is always the last to leave her restaurant. There is no backup partner for a second opinion. *Oh, come on*, she thinks as the blinking object restrains her in a choke hold. *This is Alabama, not the war zone.* She takes several deep, brain-clearing breaths and steps closer. Whatever it is, it is wedged at an angle behind the large flower pot against the back wall.

Damn, she sure needs a flashlight! No she doesn't. She could turn all the restaurant lights on. This is Gulf Shores, Alabama, not the war zone of Iraq!

She is on full alert as she unlocks the front door and steps back inside to flip the switches for all the lighting on the patio, front entrance, and parking. She closes her eyes tightly and wonders if this is a flashback from warrior days. If she looks around the door frame and the blink is gone, she will thank God of the First Baptist Church in Orange Beach and get a therapist appointment tomorrow. Sondra will also be a happy camper—happy that no one saw her in a flashback action.

She is in her soldier mode now. As she comes slowly around the door frame for a visual of the possible enemy, she sees it there. It's real, and it's still blinking.

Sondra knows from the shape and size that this device is not the normal everyday phone, iPod, or small laptop. She flips open her phone and taps in 911 just as Seth tackles her from behind. Sondra goes down hard on the brick pavers, and they both do a head roll into tables and chairs. Seth has knocked the breath out of Sondra, and she is lying so still that he thinks he may have killed her. He had never hit anyone that hard before, let alone a woman! He starts for the device, wanting to get gone fast. As he leans over to reach behind the pot for the blinking object, the now-breathing and angry Sondra the marine hits him across the back of the head with the leg from a broken chair. And he is out!

Sondra reaches over Seth and pulls out the blinking and now whining device. As she holds it, the sound turns into a timed sequence of beeps, like a bomb counting down to its explosion. She turns it toward the light to read the screen and sees that it truly is a countdown. Sondra sees a large fist out of the corner of her eye and hears a swish of air as it smashes into her chin and she is down.

The three men from Yemen grab the detonator and run for their car a half block down the street. They hear the police sirens wail, coming toward them.

The explosion is so hot and compact that the three men are incincrated as they jump into their car. Finland had programmed their device with a self destructing bomb that only they could trigger. The delegates had voted to destroy the device rather than have it in the wrong hands. Finland did not care where it was or who it was with at the time of the blast. They still had the detonator plans and a backup device.

Channel 3 News is in Gulf Shores for the Alabama College Athlete Awards presentation at the State Park Conference Center. They desert that affair for the death and arrests happening down the beach. The locals had heard the explosion, and the fire is a hot glow that lights the late-night sky for all the community to see.

The local police, state troopers, and paramedics are all over Sondra's by the Sea.

Seth is telling anyone who will listen that it is all a big mistake. Those foreigners had forced him to help them. He was innocent! The FBI, who had arrived, take Seth away in handcuffs.

Sondra has a swollen face and a black eye. She is proud to be a marine, happy this is not her life anymore, and she looks forward to getting up in the morning. Sunrise and the 5:00 a.m. fish market come early.

The End

www.ingramcontent.com/pod-product-compliance
Lightning Source LLC
Chambersburg PA
CBHW031031190726
48286CB00003BA/1123